WALL OF DAYS

Alastair Bruce

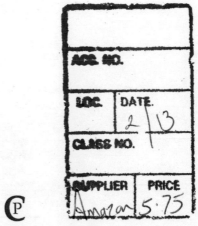

THE CLERKENWELL PRESS

First published in Great Britain in 2011 by
The Clerkenwell Press
an imprint of
PROFILE BOOKS LTD
3A Exmouth House
Pine Street
London ECIR OJH
www.profilebooks.com

First published in South Africa by
Umuzi, an imprint of Random House Struik (Pty) Ltd

1 3 5 7 9 10 8 6 4 2

Printed and bound in Great Britain by
Clays, Bungay, Suffolk

A CIP catalogue record for this book is available from the British Library.

ISBN 978 1 84668 800 3
eISBN 978 1 84765 770 1

The paper this book is printed on is certified by the © 1996 Forest Stewardship
Council A.C. (FSC). It is ancient-forest friendly. The printer holds FSC chain of custody
SGS-COC-2061

FSC
Mixed Sources
Product group from well-managed
forests and other controlled sources
Cert no. SGS-COC-2061
www.fsc.org
© 1996 Forest Stewardship Council

For Tabatha and Sophia, with love

1

It has been raining here for ten years. I keep an accurate record of time and can state this with no fear of contradiction. There have been whole days when it hasn't rained and most days it stops for a few hours. But these are pauses in a relentless fall that promises to one day submerge this island. It is already saturated in places. The marshes have doubled in size since I arrived and the cliffs to the north are falling into the bay, their mud walls no match for the rain. It is a place, this island, that is neither water nor land, an in-between world, a world in transition. When I walk through the grasslands and the marshes to the peat fields in the south I can feel the ground give way beneath my feet as if it were afloat. Sooner or later all that will be left will be the rocky hill on which I have made my home. The cave in the hill is the only place on the island that remains dry, and it is warm. I keep a fire lit and have fashioned a door, using the raft that brought me to this island.

The rain is sometimes so light it is like mist. I can see the mist creeping into the cave from below the door. It rolls in off the ocean and settles over the marshes. It swirls, eddies, faces begin to form.

At the end of each day I make a small mark with a stone on the wall of the cave. The seventh line I draw crosses the previous six. At the end of fifty-two of these plus one extra mark or two extra every fourth year I start a new row. Last night I reached the end of the tenth. Tonight I will start another. Every year with the last of the marks I remember being told why we measure time in this way – with one or two extra days in a year – but every year I realise I have forgotten the reason. I imagine it is something to do with the moon, the moon I have not seen for a decade. So much of what I do, of what we used to do, is for reasons that I cannot remember, that I dare say no one can remember.

Marks on a wall. The second time in my life I have made marks on a wall. They mean more than days. I do not forget that.

There is wood on the island. In the east is a small forest. It is a dark place. Or, darker. The light does not seem to penetrate to the floor, even though the growth is sparse. For some reason the forest has not spread. I have seen no saplings, only mature trees. I allow myself to cut down one every eight weeks. That and the peat I dig out are my sources of fuel.

I have fixed on this period of eight weeks for a simple reason. My calculations prove I have at most twenty years left on this island and at last count there were one hundred and thirty-three trees. That is approximately one every eight weeks. I have been following this practice since the seventeenth week of my arrival. In the beginning I was profligate and cut down more than I should have, before realising that none grew to take their place.

I began in the centre of the trees, in the darkest part of the small forest, and am slowly working my way out.

The peat bogs are located a mile from my cave in the direction of the forest. These too I have measured. These too I have made sure will last twenty years.

The cave, the cliffs, forest, marshlands, peat bogs – islands in a sea of wet grass. Islands within an island. One day I drew a map of the island on the wall of the cave, opposite the wall of days. The cave I marked with an X. This is my world.

I don't know if I will need twenty years. I am no longer young. In twenty years I will be seventy-three. Very few live to that age. I might well go sooner.

The island is a silent place. There is only the rain, the soft wind. When I walk through the grasslands, my hands, hanging at my sides, wipe moisture from the blades. I hear the noise of my feet in the mud and the low singing of the grass in the breeze. There are seagulls too, fewer now than in the beginning. Every now and then I find one lying in a puddle. If I find them before the worms they are usually edible. I wash them in seawater, cut off their heads, scrape out the innards. If I wrap the carcass in clay and bake it in the fire, the feathers come off with the hardened clay.

Walking through mud is hard work. It sucks you down, grasping at your ankles. Only by moving do you feel you can escape. It is mostly an illusion. The bog is treacherous if you don't know what you're doing. Some pools are deceptively deep and filled with thick mud. But I know where they are. If you didn't, and if you were weak, you could find yourself slipping into the marsh, gripped by exhaustion and cold, swallowing mouthful after mouthful of mud.

I could have built paths around the island if I had enough wood or enough stones. A path from my cave to the peat bogs, another to the forest. One to my fishing grounds, and to the northern cliffs, one circling the island. So many things I could have built. But I would need more than the island has to offer and perhaps a helper too.

I no longer talk to myself. When I first arrived it was my only way of remaining sane. Now, the sound of my voice would feel alien in the silence. If I were to talk there would be nothing to hear me, nothing save the wind, the rain, the sea. It is not a world for speech. There is no helper. I have not believed that to be a bad thing.

I do not talk also because I would imagine replies. A voice from behind a rock, behind a tree, from the top of the cliff. The speaker hidden, daring me to find him, waiting for me.

Of the two fuel sources I prefer gathering peat to chopping down trees. I cut the peat out in pieces almost the size of a man's chest: a foot long, a foot wide, a foot deep. I use a spade I brought with me to the island. I carry three pieces back with me to the cave to dry out. If they are completely dry when I use them they burn for a long time with little smoke. I use more peat than wood because there is more of it and used together in this ratio they will last twenty years. That is fortunate. It would be wrong to have to go before one's time, before being ready.

Digging peat is one of the activities on this island in which I take pleasure. There is a satisfying uniformity to the task, a mathematical precision that sits well with me. I do not think of the fact that each harvest is one step closer to the end. Rather I take pride in my work. If you could look around, you would see that I am working in a rough circle round the edges of the peat bed. At the end the spirals should be clearly visible, though perhaps the edges will have been taken over by grass, or more likely, water. From what I know about peat, this is a small bed. There is a thin layer of grass and mud to clear before you come to it and it doesn't go much deeper than a foot. Big enough for me though. Besides the neatness and simplicity of the task, I like the sound of the spade cutting through the turf. A visceral sound, more poetic than the sound of axe on wood.

Each square or tree I cut is one step closer to the end. It does not fill me with dread. I hope to be ready to go before then.

Twenty years is not such a long time. I have already been here ten. If I had taken three times as long on every task, on every step, on every axe swing and spade thrust, maybe the time would already be over. I see myself slowed down. It would make this world even quieter.

My nights here are uneventful. There is little to do after eating. By the light of the fire I fix my crab nets, mend my clothes, annotate my map. I have two journals and some ink I brought with me and it is in these journals that I record my measurements, my observations, my handwriting growing ever smaller, the rows between lines ever closer. Where I can, I use charcoal, as I have for the map of the island. For simple sums, such as the keeping of time, I use rock scraped on the walls like a caveman. Or like a convict. Both are apt descriptions of me.

Once these small tasks are done I have nothing to do but go to bed. No wine to drink, no tobacco to smoke. I lead a monk's life here.

Sometimes I have trouble sleeping. In the beginning it was difficult and lately I have been having more trouble. A sign of age. I have a technique. When it is time I close my eyes and listen. I listen for the sound of the rain, the sound of the wind, the distant waves, the gulls. I try to put other thoughts and memories to one side. Most often it works but every now and then I see faces, people behind my eyelids and the distant cry of a gull turns into the scream of a child and I am wide awake, chilled to the core.

I repair my nets and do my sums, scratch time on the walls of my cave. I sleep, when I can, from soon after sunset till sunrise and when I am awake I keep myself busy. I cannot do otherwise. I do not have to survey the island to the extent that I have. I do not have to be so meticulous about the peat and the forests. I could gorge myself, build up the fire, dry everything out, heat water for a wash. But I will not let go of certain standards by which I have lived my life. I swim in the sea every morning, eat, usually the remains of the previous night's meal, and after that collect fuel. The afternoon I spend fishing or gathering food of some variety. There are a few edible leaves and tubers in the forest, seeds from the grasses, fungi. These, along with fish, crabs, seagulls, tubers and worms, are what sustain me.

When I walk on the shoreline I keep my head down, looking for crabs and dead fish. If I see a new species of fish or crustacean and it is relatively fresh, I put it in my bag for closer inspection in the cave. Once I have examined it I eat it if I think it will not make me ill. So far I have been lucky, aside from the three varieties of fungus that made me nauseous. There is an area where kelp washes ashore. I cut pieces of this to take back as well. You can place shellfish in the tube and put it near a hot fire. The shellfish steams inside and comes out tender and tasting of the ocean. It is one of my few treats on the island.

Cooking in kelp is something I learned years ago. We were in the north-west sailing down the coast of another island in our small boats, returning from a campaign to find fertile land. That is all our world seems to consist of: a few islands separated by vast oceans. Some are deserts, some dead swamps, most are uninhabitable. Only a few are capable of supporting any life. We had found nothing. Most of the force was dead and we were being harried by the enemy. My men were hungry. The shoreline until then had been barren but that night we put to shore near a rocky stretch of beach and I sent a few men to see what they could find. They came back with a feast gleaned from the rocks and proceeded to cook it in kelp. It was unusual to find food like that and it turned out to be the last meal we had for days. As many of us died from starvation and illness as from the spears, arrows and guns of the enemy.

Once I have gathered food I check my fresh-water supply. I have three containers for water. There are no streams on the island but collecting water is easy. In a place where it never stops raining it would be hard to die of thirst. I have built up a circle of stones and hung a cloth over the top. The centre of the cloth is lower than the edges. I place one of the containers under the cloth. Most days it overflows.

When I have enough food and water I turn to my studies of the island. I am categorising the plants and animals here. So far I have counted five varieties of fish, two anemones, seaweed, limpets, two types of crab, seven types of fungus, four edible, three that cause nausea, three different types of grass, one type of tree, eight other plants, one species of gull and one of worm.

There isn't much life on the island. There are no rats, no rabbits, no moles. The gulls are disappearing and there is no other birdlife. But that is commonplace and it is a small island. Cut off. It has probably been cut off for thousands of years unlike most islands I know, which appear to have been created in a more recent past.

I have trodden every inch of this island from the cliffs through the grasslands, through the forest to the peat beds and then around the island on the rocky and muddy coast, passing the fishing bay and the wilder eastern shore. You can cover a lot of ground in ten years. I have touched every rock, every plant, peered behind every tree and into every rock pool. I have tasted its roots, its water, its life. It holds fewer and fewer surprises for me. We are old companions.

I am measuring the island's coastline, a difficult task when part of it slips into the sea every day. I am preoccupied with getting my representation of the island to scale and keeping it to scale, rubbing out charcoal outlines when I have to.

To make a complete circuit of the island, which is now around fifteen miles in circumference, takes four hours. I can mostly walk around on the beach or the rocks if the tide is right. If it is in when I reach the northern cliffs I have to climb them and leave the coast for a while. This adds half an hour to the walk. Of course, if I do my measurements it can take longer.

When I arrived the island was larger in circumference, about eighteen miles. I have lost three miles in ten years. If it continues at the same rate the island will last another fifty years. But it won't. As the island's circumference decreases, the relative area exposed to the sea and the elements increases, thereby speeding up erosion. The cliffs are disappearing more quickly now than ten years ago, more quickly today than yesterday. When the marshlands are breached by the sea, the process will speed up further and the island will disappear in no time at all. I have toyed with the idea of building a dyke and in fact I spent a month working on it a few years back but I have given up on the idea. The island is not mine to control. It will disappear one day and then I must go too, if I have not gone already. The end of both our histories.

The idea that a circle diminishes in size more quickly the smaller it gets is one that I think about often. I have spent evenings working out the rate of acceleration and so pinpointing the time when the island will disappear. Twenty years is the figure I have come up with. Twenty years from now the island will still be here but of a size no longer able to sustain me. I would spend my last minutes draped across the island, my toes in the southern ocean, my fingers in the northern. At least, that is how it will feel.

In truth, I don't know whether this is correct. I am not a mathematician and I have no one to check my sums. The more I think about it the less obvious the idea is. You could argue that the smaller the island gets the slower it will disappear. Today it is shrinking less rapidly than yesterday, less than the day before. Perhaps there will come a time when the island will stop shrinking completely and it will go on and on long after I have withered away.

So, I fill my time this way. And it is a good use of my time. When I am gone I will leave a record for future generations, if there are any. It may be a small thing on a small island in a forgotten part of the world but I will leave a legacy, I will leave a history of this place.

There is something else I marked on my map. Somewhere else I visit. About three years into my time here and for the next two-and-a-half years, every day at dusk I would take a stone about three times the size of my fist and place it in an area of the grasslands where little that is edible grows. The day after I'd place one next to it. After a row of thirty I'd start another. Thirty-one rows, the last with just seventeen stones in it. Each day for nine hundred and seventeen days. And now each day I go back. It does not look like many. It looks almost insignificant, my stone field. Each day I stand and watch the stones splashed with rain. They reflect the clouds. In the dusk, with my head bowed, eyes half closed, each stone becomes alive, becomes a spirit. They swim around me, swallow me, pull me down into the grey water.

A story I have heard tells of a black smoke covering the earth. People were born in it, breathed it, died in it. It went on for so long people forgot why it was there, if they ever knew in the first place. Many lived underground, became smaller, nourished by roots and a foul soil. Slowly they started coming out. Some died trapped between the dark air and the suffocating earth. I pictured them with their legs held in soil, their arms lifted to the sky. Others woke and in the grey light the earth began to move. But it is just a story.

I imagine, standing here, the shapes around me, that this is what it must have been like for them. The half light, the not being able to breathe.

This place is on the very edge of the territories called Bran. Somewhere to the east lies Axum, its only rival and the only other settlement the world knows.

There are rumours, legends of something and somewhere else. There are measurements for space and time we didn't determine, there are words for things that no one has experienced, there are things we believe to be true but cannot prove. I write that I lead a monk's life. The world does not know monks, yet I know the word and I know, or believe I know it describes a man who lives ascetically. We have plastic, have the word for plastic but do not produce it or know how to produce it. We know the north and south are uninhabitable but cannot remember how they got that way. The story of the smoke. Scraps of knowledge, scraps of collective memories. There are stories of a time with many more of us, a time of plenty. But they were over long before our story starts and long before I can remember. My role in Bran meant that I have seen more, that I have seen things very few of my people would believe. An enormous ship half buried in a desert. Ruined buildings at the bottom of a lake. All these clues to our past we could not read for fear of what they might mean, for fear of what they might mean we used to be. I have seen so much that hints of a past greater than our present. But we were never ready for the past. The present was struggle enough.

On the way here, a week's sail into the trip, the sea became like glass. I looked over the edge of the raft and could see metres down. I spent ages peering over, seeing nothing, just water. And then dark shapes appeared. I drifted across them. Some reached upwards and I could see ruins, outlines of buildings, the spaces between them. I drifted over a column that came almost to the surface. On the top of the column was a statue of a man. I reached into the water up to my shoulder, straining to touch him. He wore a hat. He had the bearing of a military man. His face was expressionless, his visage stone. My fingertips brushed the top of his head and he was gone. The ocean swallowed him. Once more, and ever more, undisturbed, unseen. I drifted onwards.

I have been left alone here. No one ventures far north or south. Bran is to the west, Axum to the east. The borders of the two settlements, themselves islands, though much larger than this one, are not patrolled. We did not have the resources and probably do not now either and when I left there had been no intrusions into our region for years. The two factions left each other alone. We left each other to get on with it. For a time there were ambassadors sent to each other's regions to ensure the Programme was being carried out in accordance with the terms of the peace agreement. Gradually though, as it became apparent how well the Programme was working, how good it was for both groups, there was no need to monitor each other.

That was a long time ago. As I sit here fishing, the rain falling softly on my waterproof cover, I feel it may as well not have happened at all. The rain on the plastic is a sound that is comforting. I am warm, I have food, I have found a way to live.

I picture myself here as if from a distance: a man crouched on a wet rock, under a yellow tarpaulin, a fishing rod reaching out into the sea. Behind him the sand, the crumbling cliffs, grasslands and an immense expanse of grey sky. I'm standing on the cliff, looking down at me, looking out at the ocean, and this is what I see.

There is a tug on the line and I am back, flying over the edge of the cliff.

The fish is a strong one. It will be all I need for two days. I reel it in, take a rock and hit it on the head. I gut it there and then, placing my knife just below its jaw and slicing down with a single movement. I have done this many times before. The innards I pull out with my fingers and fling to a lone seagull perched on a rock. I wash the cavity in the sea and place the fish in my bag.

As I stand up and turn towards the path leading up the cliff, something catches my eye. I see it disappear behind the ridge. For a few seconds I am startled and think I have seen a head. It doesn't last long. I realise I am not sure what I saw, whether I saw anything in fact. There have been other times like this. I've seen things. They're becoming more frequent. But it must have been grass blowing in the wind, a gull, or simply an old man's fading eyesight. I set off up the path to the cave.

At night I think back to the creature on the ridge. It changes at night. It always does. The head becomes a face, a face with bones visible through holes in the skin and drawn teeth.

I do not sleep and wait for dawn. It is one of those mornings when it is lighter than usual. Each day is a shade of grey. It can range from near white to almost black. I have not seen the sun for ten years but every now and then I can see a flame-white disc through the clouds. Today is one of those days. I swim, I eat, I pull on my coat and head off to gather fuel.

The coat, spare clothes, a knife, a length of rope, waterproofs, fishing line and hooks, a tarpaulin used for a sail, water containers, biscuits, some twine, a spare set of boots, a spade, an axe, my writing materials, a compass and an old chart of the ocean. This is what they allowed me. This is what I brought to the island and what I have with me now, some of it repaired several times.

I had to replace the handle of my axe a few months after I arrived. The original broke while I was chopping down a tree. It didn't splinter.

It snapped clean in two. My hand, carried through with the movement of my arm, scraped against the broken shaft. It cut deep into the tops of my fingers. I held them up to the light and for a second could see bone before the blood came. I bled profusely and watched as it dripped into the earth. There was nothing I could do. A needle and thread were not on my list of provisions. I was surprised at how much it bled. The dark forest closed in, I smelled the damp pine needles, the fresh wood, heard my own quickened breathing, the silence, felt the warmth of the blood on my skin. There was nothing I could do to stop myself bleeding to death, nothing I could do to live. But it was a cut across the fingers and no one has ever died from that. I tore a strip of cloth from my shirt and wound it round my hand.

After the bleeding had stopped I walked to the shore and washed the wound in seawater. It stung for a bit but not much. I sat on the rocks for a long time, staring out to sea. I was thinking of how I had reacted. Even if only for a minute I was afraid. When I first set foot on this shore I set to work straight away. I knew what I had to do and I did it. I knew the island could support me and the thought of a life without other people was something I had already had some time to get used to. And I was never a sociable person. But this, now. I did not know what to think. It was then that I stopped talking to myself, then that the island became quieter. Long ago, in island time.

The handle I fashioned has worked a charm since then. It is perhaps not as smooth as the first, not as easy to grip but it is mine. It is now worn to my touch and feels right in my hand. Every time I use it though I remember the day the first one broke.

The forest is not my favourite place on the island. Everyone has a place like this in the areas in which they move. No matter how much you love where you live there is always a dark corner, always somewhere you would prefer not to go. I have my head down, breathing heavily, the thud of the axe echoing around the pines. I feel out of place. I feel surrounded. The noise of the final splintering of the trunk always takes me by surprise. I glance around whenever a tree falls as if I think someone is watching. I look up to see if there is a body in the branches. But I know there is no one to watch me. If I close my eyes in that place, shapes appear behind my eyelids. When I leave the forest and step out into the light I feel the breeze drying my sweat. It makes me shiver.

At the end of the day, I draw another line on the wall.

When I first arrived I toyed with the idea of naming the island, of putting up a sign facing out to the ocean in case someone came looking for me. But I gave up on the idea. It is better off without a name. And what would I have called it anyway? A name for a place without a history would be pointless.

It is raining heavily when I make my way down to the shore for my swim. I take nothing with me and I walk down the cliff path naked. When I first came here I felt self-conscious about doing that. Now I don't think much about it. It keeps my clothes dry and, besides, it is never unbearably cold here. My feet have toughened up and I don't feel the small stones under my soles.

There is a reef about half a mile out and it is to there I swim, to where I can feel the spray from the breakers on my face. The spray and, in between, the drops of rain. The ocean is warm, the rain cold. I float in the water on my back, tasting the salt, before starting slowly back.

Today when I reach the shore and am standing catching my breath I see something further down the coast. Nothing has ever washed up here, nothing besides dead fish and birds. I can't tell what it is but it is a dark red colour and looks out of place on the grey sand. I walk over and as I get closer I realise it is a coat, a man's coat, soaked through, torn and covered in marine snails. I shake them off and hold it up to the light.

I go through how this could have appeared. I have gone so long without seeing anything washed up and then this, so out of place. The routes we once sailed on our way to war were far to the north and, since a couple of years after the peace, were unused. No one bothers to try to fish from boats anymore. What little fish there are gather mostly round the shorelines. A man can be in a boat for days and not catch a single fish. I was lucky to catch a few on the way over here. When I left Bran we had been talking about sending ships on exploratory voyages, looking for regions we had forgotten about, regions whose climate had changed for the better. Perhaps these have begun. But here? Sailing so close to Axum is tantamount to a declaration of war under the terms of the Peace Treaty. Perhaps a ship was lost, the crew hungry, its captain uncertain and losing influence. There was a mutiny, the captain hurled overboard, his possessions shared amongst the men. Except for the coat, lost overboard in a scuffle.

Or is this the remains of another exile? A piece of flotsam from a forgotten world.

I shiver. I look around me. I don't know if I expect to see someone.

I think of the shadows over the horizon, the eyes staring after me. I watch the mist rolling in. A gull calls.

Suddenly I am flying again. I look down on a man clutching a red coat. I scan the island. The higher I am the more of it I can see but the less detail I can make out. Is that a rock or a man in the shadows of the cliff face? A dip in the grass or a body pressed down to avoid being seen? I cannot tell. It grows darker and the figure with the red coat on the shore fades with the mist and the last of the light.

2

In the cave I spread the coat out on a rock. I sit opposite it and pick at my food. I have not dried myself.

The coat looks like it is part of a uniform. Stained red. Metal buttons. It is not from Bran. It is not something one of my people would wear. The uniform of our soldiers was brown.

It takes me back.

I remember killing a man. A man who wore a coat like this, though plainer, less well made. I remember killing many, both as soldier and later but this one in particular. We had surrounded a house in a burnt-out settlement. Whether it had burned in recent fighting or decades before I don't know. We had tracked an enemy platoon which was taking cover in the ruins. Our orders were to storm the house where the soldiers were hiding and kill the occupants. We were not able to look after prisoners. Our charity extended to refugees but not to the enemy. I went in through the front door, others went in through windows, through gaps in walls. They did not stand a chance. The enemy got off three shots. Three between seven of them. One was too scared to shoot. He stood in the corner, still holding his rifle but flinching at the sounds of the shots. No one but me seemed to notice him. I kept an eye on him during the few seconds of fighting. When the others were dead I shouted to stop firing. I walked up to him. He was a boy. He was not crying. His body was turned slightly away from me, fearing a strike. He fixed his eyes on my chin. My gun was aimed at him. I flicked my head at him, meaning he should turn around. I watched his breathing slow down and he nodded. He understood. That stayed with me and I saw it many times after that. I told him to kneel. With my gun still at his head I reached down to his belt. I took his knife from him. We were not allowed to waste bullets. If you could you had to kill people in other ways. I holstered my gun. I took his forehead in my left hand. With the knife in my right I drew a line across his throat. I did it rapidly but I felt each tendon, felt each muscle sever. He did not make a sound. I let him go and he fell to the ground. The rest may have been slightly different but the nod I remember. The moment fear turned to acceptance. I kept the knife. A lifetime later I still have it.

That was early on in the wars, which would drag on for another eleven years. By the end I was leader of the entire force: a thousand men.

The wars largely fought themselves out. We kept on killing each other, kept on dying, until our populations were reduced to a level where the land could begin to sustain us all. We negotiated a peace, the terms of which ensured sustainability. I say 'we'; it was I who brokered the peace, along with my counterpart from the other side. It was a tense peace and not without sadness, not without consequences, but peace nonetheless. It lasted until I left and probably beyond.

I remember saying goodbye to Bran. A few people had accompanied the soldiers and me to the coast. There were a few civil servants, the judge, my neighbours and of course the new Marshal, my successor and protégé, Abel. My lover was there too, though by that stage I could not call her that.

The Marshal would not look me in the eye. Instead he looked over my shoulder. His lips were a thin line. I remember the touch of his hand as he briefly shook mine. It was soft – the grip, the skin. No doubt mine was too. The life of a Marshal in our outpost was not a physically demanding one. In years gone by we were fighters. But peace made us softer. It gave us more time for contemplation, more time to consider what we did.

I imagine the people on the mainland, those I have left behind. They stand on the rocky beach in the sun staring out to sea, the waves lapping at their feet. I wonder what they might be thinking. I wonder, if we could see far enough, if we would wave to each other or whether we would simply stare in silence. But no one can see that far. I was on the raft for three weeks before putting to shore here.

Many of my people I can no longer picture. I have memories involving them but their figures are a blur, fading pictures, ghosts. They talk, they gesture but I cannot see their eyes.

The woman though, her I can remember. She was not particularly beautiful. She was thirty-five when I left but looked older. I think we all did. A lifetime working in the kitchens, washing up, standing for twelve hours a day had aged her. She had hands that were callused and dull skin. Her eyes though, when she looked at you, stared through you. There was no hiding from her. To have someone truly know you is to be complete no matter what it is they know, even if what they know is the darkest thing of all.

We had been seeing each other for twelve years. We would spend

Wednesday nights together, her night off. That was almost the only time we could see each other. I worked during the day, she finished late at night. We missed only two Wednesdays during those years. The first time was my fault, although there was little I could do about it. I was at a peace conference with the leader of Axum – there were plenty of men there in coats like this – finalising the details of the Programme. The second time was because of the death of her mother. She told me she needed some time alone. I did not expect to see her again. I thought that what I had done might preclude this. But the following week there was a knock at the door at seven, our time, and it was her. I could tell she was sad and she was distant from me but to see her back made my heart leap. I could not share this with her. I could not. How could I? She stood in the doorway, would not look at me and said simply, 'We will not talk about her.' I nodded. And we did not.

The woman's name was Tora. She lived in a flat close to the kitchens. It was small, basically furnished but always clean with nothing out of place. In her bedroom there was a bed, a dark wooden wardrobe and a dresser. I do not know whether she cleaned the flat when she knew I was coming or whether it was always tidy. I suppose I will never know.

Two years into our relationship I asked her to move in with me and to make it official. She refused. I did not understand why at first. She said it was unnecessary. I never asked again and I grew to understand what she meant. We had all we needed and all we wanted. Any more would have thrown the balance out. She was a level-headed woman, a quality I admired. She did keep me at a certain distance throughout but perhaps the pressures of our time meant that very few people were capable of deep feeling.

When we were together in bed she would close her eyes and bite her lower lip. The final time I closed mine too as I could not bear to look at her, as I could not bear to look. There was a chasm between us.

I did not know for certain it would be the last time but the trial had not been going well and I was expecting it not to go my way. In the end the sentence was not death but worse. It was banishment for life, a death in life. A life in death.

And she was no longer completely with me by then.

I suppose I had my standing to thank for not being executed and perhaps a sense of complicity. When I left, sailing away from the beach, I fixed my eyes on them willing them to look. Very few of them did. A minor triumph.

My relationship with Tora, while not exactly frowned upon by the townspeople, was viewed as unconventional. But it did not cause many problems. The rest of my life was conventional. I performed my duties rigorously, kept in touch with my lieutenants, wore my medals on the anniversaries of key battles and the peace agreement and saw the same woman for twelve years at the same time in the same place. I had routine.

I cultivated the aloofness that people sensed. With the role I had to fill it was a necessity. Even when I ran for the position of Marshal on the back of the Programme, the big idea, and I managed to persuade three-quarters of the population to back me, I knew that it was not me they were voting for, it was not me they were following. It was the order I could bring, the promise of an end to needless killing.

I was never a man of the people. Even Abel, the person I spent most time with, I kept at a distance. I think he preferred it that way though. He was not exactly jovial either. I went to his house a few times on social calls but not many. I introduced him to Tora. We were walking by the kitchens, Tora was outside sitting in the sun. It was early in our relationship. I went up to her and kissed her. I was uncertain what to do, I will admit, with Abel looking on. She leant away from me a little. I introduced her to Abel and we went on our way.

Once after this he asked me if I would like to bring someone with me when I visited him. I said no. We did not mention her again.

On the beach that day I kissed her again. Everyone was watching. There was no noise from them, no disrespect. They just watched. My going was a quiet affair. Everyone wanted me gone but everyone knew the role they themselves had played. For the most part people stayed in their houses, stayed in the town, while the old Marshal was put on a boat with the most basic of provisions and implements.

I kissed her. This time she did not pull away. I am still grateful.

About half a mile off the coast I looked around at them for the last time. The two of them, Abel and Tora, were left. They had half turned towards each other. They may have been talking. I still wonder what they were saying.

When I kissed her she smelt of the harsh soap they used on dishes. I can smell it now.

I wonder if the townspeople would recognise me. I have a beard and long hair. I cut the hair occasionally but it is impossible to get a close shave using just a knife. I am also brown, like the island, and lean. Though I eat regularly it is not the sort of food that puts meat on your bones. In Bran I grew pale from a mostly sedentary life and slightly overweight, a flabby man living a soft life. Though we did not have much food, it was often very filling. Now though, I have broader shoulders, strong legs and carry no extra weight. Altogether a fitter man.

They might have wanted me to die on the way here. There is no guilt if a man drowns alone miles from anywhere. But I didn't. I survived. I drank dew and rainwater. Ate seaweed. I caught some fish. Once I pulled a dead one from the surface of the barren ocean. I arrived on the island and have eked a living from it. Alone. I imagine people. I imagine others. Faces of others. Voices. But I know they are not real. I know they are not alive.

But now this coat. It has been worn recently. Food and fuel will have to wait today. I must set out on a tour of the island. I have to check if I am still alone.

I have been sitting in the cave for a long time and it is afternoon by the time I set out. After just over an hour of walking the cliffs come into view. They would be close enough to see from much further off but you have to round a bluff. It is an impressive sight, at least by the standards of this island. They stand vast, grey and crumbling, like a derelict monument to a forgotten leader. Though their decay represents the erosion of my time here, I feel awe, not trepidation, when I'm near them. The sea around the cliffs is tainted with the mud and is always rough. I sometimes think it looks like blood.

The tide is out today. The sea has retreated leaving a long strip of grey beach. The tides are extreme here. In a few hours the waves will be beating against the cliffs from below, the rain more gently from above. Out along the strand I see a much paler object, so pale it is almost white. A rock perhaps. But it is different to any I have seen on the island before.

I begin the climb down to the beach.

A few minutes later and I am closer, my eyes fixed on the object.

I slow down, stop walking. I know what it is now. Now I can hear only the wind. The wind and the waves. Everything has slowed down. Stopped. I breathe in, which seems to take minutes. I pick up a rock and I am moving again. I run towards the mound. Stop again. Run. I veer off towards some boulders and crouch behind them, my eyes still fixed on it. My breathing is quicker now. It comes in rasps like it does when I have been chopping wood. It does not move.

I watch for minutes. The rain falls in swathes along the beach. I feel it run into my eyes and down the back of my neck. The rain is heavy and sometimes he disappears behind curtains of water. I have to wipe the rain from my eyes to see him properly.

It is the first person I have seen for a decade. He is large, bulging with fat. Not a working man. His face is turned away from me. He is lying on his stomach, feet turned in towards each other, his palms upwards. He has no hair. A white whale, and possibly a dead white whale.

The coat must belong to him.

In the last ten years I have seen only shadows. This is different, so solid, so unlike a mirage. I blink, holding my eyes closed for seconds. Each time I open them he is still there.

I walk out slowly from behind the rocks. I open my mouth to speak. No words come. It is as if I have forgotten how. I try again. This time it is a breath, just louder than the wind. I swallow and try once more. Finally the word comes out. 'Hello.' It is a whisper, a croak. Again. The word is no more than a grunt. It still does not sound like the word I know it is. He does not move. I am now three metres away from him. I walk in a circle around him, keeping the same distance, my hand still clutching the rock. A dog with its prey. I can see only part of his face.

He is clean-shaven with heavy jowls and a double-chin. His eyes are closed. From his face I know he is not dead.

I crouch down on my haunches and watch his face closely. He is breathing. His bulk rises every few seconds and his lips part when he exhales. He seems peaceful. A man dozing on a beach.

His fat fingers rest on the sand. White worms in black mud. He is covered in drops of water, the rain or the sea. They glisten in the last of the light.

I raise myself, walk up to him and prod him in the ribs with my foot. He does not move. I lean down and shake him roughly by the shoulder. He is as cold as stone. His eyelids open. The eyes are red, the irises dark, almost black. For a few seconds he does not move. Suddenly he takes fright, tries to shuffle away from me, using his arms to shift his bulk. He cannot lift himself. His breathing quickens. I hold up my hands to show I mean no harm and take a step back. I do not speak. Instead I crouch down again so I don't tower over him. This seems to relax him slightly and his breathing becomes more regular. We look at each other. I can still only see half his face.

After a few moments I say again, 'Hello.' I can recognise the word now but my tongue feels thick in my mouth. He does not respond. I introduce myself. I do not know what name to give myself, my military title or just my birth-name. I decide on both. 'I am Bran. Marshal. I live here.'

I realise I am speaking in short bursts. I have to get used to talking. His eyes give nothing away. I am not sure he has even heard me. I try again. 'Where are you from? Axum.' It is more a statement than a question.

Still nothing. 'You are safe. Talk.'

The man closes his eyes. He may be in shock. I have no idea what he might have endured. I place my coat over him to keep him warm. As I lean closer I catch his scent. He smells of the sea. Not the pleasant smell.

We do not have much time. The tide is out but there are just a couple of hours before it comes in and if we are caught here we would both drown. And the light is fading. I can let him sleep for just a short while before we need to start walking back the way I have come. There is accessible higher ground half a mile away. I know I will in all likelihood have to half carry him as he looks weak. I set off for the higher ground taking my bag with me so I will have nothing else to carry when I return.

When I do it is dark. I find him in the same position. I wake him again. 'You will drown here.' Though he does not reply he seems to understand and tries to lift himself. I place my hand under his arms and haul him up. He stumbles against me, his legs without strength. He makes me think of a white grub, one whose only purpose in life is feeding. I ignore my distaste and place his arm across my shoulders and my arm under his. Like this we walk slowly along the beach. At one point I smile to myself at the picture we make. To a creature flying above us, or staring down from the grass ridge, or pressed back into the black mud of the cliffs, we would make an odd couple indeed. One tall and stringy, weathered brown, half carrying the other, a stumbling and bloated man, in the dark, pale as the rain.

It is raining hard now. There is some light from the moon behind the clouds but it is faint.

I resign myself to a night of cold and wet. With no fire, no hot food, it is simply a case of waiting out the rain, waiting for dawn.

I shuffle up the last section of the cliff and walk a hundred metres inland to a grassy area with the man still hanging on to me. I let him down. He now seems asleep or unconscious. My grip slips on his wet skin. He falls into a puddle and lands with his face in the water, mud splashing onto his cheek. An eye and part of his mouth are under water. He splutters, tries to move but can't shift his bulk. I watch him gag. I am breathing heavily from the strain. He lets out a gurgled cry. Not a mute then. I take his arm and turn him over. 'I will build shelter,' I say to him. 'I have food. We will sleep.' He looks blankly at me.

I spend the night shivering, clasping my arms around me, and sleep little. The man sits across from me leaning against a rock. He seems not to mind the cold and sits watching me, expressionless. When I wake, after drifting off for what seems like just a few minutes, he is still staring at me, his black eyes unblinking. It is dark but I am close enough to see his eyes. I can smell him too. It is not something I am used to, another human's smell. The smell of wet grass, mud, rotting birds, pine from the forest, the sometimes dank smell of the peat smoke: these I am used to, these have become mine, my smell, a smell of an island man. But his, an odour of the decaying ocean, wet skin, almost sweet but distastefully so, his is alien.

As it grows lighter and his face comes into focus, I have a feeling I recognise him. I search my memory. I cannot place him.

'Hello,' I try again. My voice is coming back. 'I am Bran. I live on this island. What is your name?' He is still looking at me but says nothing.

'Who are you? How did you come here?' I feel myself growing annoyed at the silence.

'What are you? Axumite?' I ask again. 'What were you there?' I sigh when he still does not respond and look away through the opening of the tent.

'You have had a hard time. I understand. You do not have to talk to me now.' I am annoyed but I have a duty to this man. He is on my island. He is my responsibility. 'There is a cave on the other side of the island. It is where I live. It is warm. I can make a fire and cook. We must go now. It will take hours to get there.' I know this will be a difficult trip back. I now have all my gear to carry and can see that he is no stronger than yesterday so I will be supporting him as well.

I get to my feet and begin to gather up the canvas. He does not move and I drag it over him as if he wasn't there. I put the bag on my shoulders, walk behind him and, without a word, lift him up from his armpits. He is a dead weight and when he gets to his feet he totters unsteadily. I hold him by the arm. 'Can you walk?' At that he tries to walk, takes a few steps but his legs shake and I take him by the arm again.

Like this we make our way slowly back to the cave, stopping every few minutes to rest. I am tired too, having barely eaten for two days. By the time we make it back it is early afternoon. I have to forego collecting fuel. There is a small store of it but it won't last long.

In the cave I look again at him. I search my memories. Something there I cannot find.

I build up the fire, place him on my bed, take my fishing gear and head off down the path, closing the door behind me.

My mind wanders as I fish. I almost miss a tug on the line. I find myself making up stories that could explain this man's presence. An ambassador from Axum sent to re-establish contact with Bran. A refugee. A man from an undiscovered part of the world, a place lost for centuries, untouched by our wars, our famines, our destructive climates. A place of dragons and legendary kings. He has walked up from the bottom of the ocean, half man, half fish. Buried in the mud of the cliffs for ages, released now by the waves, he has been brought back to life by the warm rains. My imagination knows no bounds. A killer. A man from who knows where driven by vengeance and greed and lust for death. A silent man, plotting even now to take over my island. Or, like me, an exile, a visionary, a leader of men fallen foul of changing sentiment, banished to take his chance on the high seas. More sinned against than sinning. I allow my mind to wander too much.

Considering his size, the coat, the softness of his flesh, he is most likely a senior figure in Axum.

Perhaps still a criminal though. But then I too, in law, am one.

I think about him in the cave and wonder what he is doing. My back is to the cliff. I begin to feel his eyes staring at me from the ridge. I look around quickly. There is nothing to be seen.

And then I know.

And then I know who he is. It comes to me. It has been over twenty years since I last saw him and he has changed so much and I hadn't got a clear look at him until this morning. That is why it has taken me so long. I jump up, turn as if to run to him but sit down again. There is no reason to let him realise I know who he is just yet. I need to see if I can discover his intentions, to see if I can make him talk.

His name is Andalus. He was ruler of Axum. A senior leader indeed. He is the man with whom I concluded peace for our territories, the man with whom I formulated the Programme, though it was mostly

36

my idea. I am surprised he is here. Very surprised. It is potentially a bad omen. I will have to find out his story and to do that I will have to keep my knowledge of his identity secret and hope he doesn't recognise me.

I hook a second fish. They are both small but enough for one night. At the cave I cook them with some roots I place near the fire. The outside of the root becomes charred but the inside remains soft. I don't know what it is but it tastes like sweet potato. When I give him the food he eats hungrily, quickly. It is the quickest I have seen him move since I found him. I am surprised he does not burn his mouth. He finishes long before I do and I give him some of mine. While he eats I watch him and the memories come back. Beneath the bulk, somewhere within this fat grub of a man is my enemy, my enemy who became a friend, of sorts. Under a changed skin is a link to what I am, to what I was.

We eat all the food and by the time we finish it is dark again and we settle in for our second night.

He is still sleeping when I leave the cave the next morning. He lies on his side, curled up like a baby. I am concerned that my routine has been put out. If I am to feed him I will have to collect more fuel and harvest or catch more food. I will have to work more quickly. I take my clothes with me when I go swimming and head straight to the peat beds from there.

When Tora came to me on that Wednesday evening after the death of her mother, I knew then that we would last. And we did; until near the end. As I held her – she did not then hold me back – I had to take a couple of sharp breaths to avoid making a sound. I don't know if she felt these. I knew because if a relationship can survive that it can survive almost anything. I did not think of asking her to join me in exile. I suspect Abel would have vetoed it but it was not a question I would have asked. For all I knew when I left the settlement I would be dead in a matter of days. No, I did not want Tora with me. I do wonder what she would have said but, truth is, she most likely would have said no. She had moved on, though I suspect she still harboured feelings for me. I have no regrets. If she had been here the supplies would have to be divided in two, making our time together shorter. And if we had had a child it would be shorter still. There comes a point at which, if I had been a patriarch with a content wife and several children, the birth of a further child would cut our time down to hours. Perhaps even, though this is mathematically impossible, a birth would cause time to regress, to go backwards and we would already be dead. We would never have existed.

This man I have found, he will cut down my time here but at least it will end there. At least he is only one variable.

Back in the cave I find he has not moved.

I address him: 'Are you ready to tell me why you are here?' His eyes are open but he is unblinking. He has shown no signs of recognising me. 'I will need help collecting food and fuel.' He does not reply. I am beginning to grow impatient but I will give him some more time. He is a guest after all. And an acquaintance. Through the war and beyond we Brans maintained a spirit of generosity, though in the time of the Programme it had little chance to show itself.

In spite of having little food we always catered for refugees who continued to trickle in during and after the war. We absorbed the healthy ones into our society where we could, absorbed them into the rationing system. The populace weren't allowed food in their homes since communal cooking cut down on waste. So we would stand in a queue with these refugees, these people who had given nothing to us, and they would be fed the same as everyone else, the same as the healthy at least.

I decide to head back to the beach to fish instead of collecting grass seeds and roots. Fish will help Andalus get his strength back more quickly.

The seeds I mash and boil into a gruel of sorts. It is less appetising than fish but if I am to eke out every moment of the island's life I need a balanced diet. I look after myself in this way. I fear there will not be enough time to collect seeds if I have to catch twice as many fish. If I fall behind and cannot collect enough food I will lose strength and grow weaker faster and I might never be able to get out of the spiral. The balance would be thrown out.

I have been able to smoke fish but in the damp it is difficult to store food and the worms and insects seem able to find whatever I leave out. I have tried eating these worms too but they are vile and I would rather eat the food that attracts them.

I could keep a fire going in the cave. Eventually the moisture on the walls would go and it would be dry but to do that I would exhaust my fuel supplies very quickly.

I catch four small fish this time. They are like the ones I used to enjoy as a young man but have a sharper nose and a slightly gamier taste. I call them Species Three as they are the third variety I caught. The task of naming I leave to others. I check my crab nets, which are located nearby. One contains a couple of crabs and I remove these carefully.

Andalus is sitting on the floor when I get back to the cave. 'Who are you?' I ask. He does not speak. I walk up to him. He has his back to me. I whisper, 'Who are you?' I bend down and whisper even more softly in his ear, 'I can guess, if that's the way you want to play it. I can guess your name.' He does not move. He still appears not to recognise me. I step away and walk round to face him. I hold up the fish. 'Do you know what to do with these?' I have not yet gutted them. 'You can nod or shake your head. You do not have to talk.' He does not move. 'I will give you a knife. You place the point here,' I show him where I mean, 'and draw the blade downwards like this. You must do this so we can eat.' I realise I am talking to him as if to a child.

I place the fish on the ground, take his hand and wrap his fingers round the knife handle. He grips it tightly but makes no move to take the fish. I notice his knuckles grow whiter. I step away from him. I am not afraid. Though he is bigger than I am, he is slow and weak and as a former soldier I am used to hand-to-hand combat. I am in fact intrigued to see what he will do. But he makes no effort to get up and after a minute loosens his grip. The knife slips to the floor. As he drops it the blade slices one of his fingers. A drop of blood falls onto the fish. 'Hold it up,' I say. 'It will stop soon enough.' He obeys. As I sit in the entrance to the cave gutting the fish I am aware he does not lower it. He looks as if he is frozen mid-sentence emphasising a point. I smile to myself.

Tora's mother was sixty-eight when she died. It is a good age. She kept working until the end, maintaining a small garden adjacent to the city walls. One day she did not get out of bed. When Tora found her later that evening she was barely able to move or talk. It was a death

sentence. Her garden was taken over, she said her goodbyes and Tora moved on. There was little time to grieve.

I knew her mother quite well. I assigned her the garden, which she loved. It was a tiny patch but was managed efficiently and everyone had to do something. She grew potatoes, squash and had a small orange tree. She would sit out of the sun under the tree at the end of the day talking to her neighbours, her fellow gardeners. I would pass by on occasion and exchange pleasantries. I suspect she did not like me very much. She was always polite, given I had procured this work for her, I was seeing her daughter and I was Marshal, but we never progressed beyond conversations about her vegetables and the weather. We never spoke about Tora.

I miss her more than some of the others, it must be said. I think of her often. She is a symbol of what I might have become. I would have enjoyed retiring, spending my afternoons in the sun, tending my vegetable patch and thinking of the past only to reminisce with acquaintances. It is the sun I miss most, falling asleep in the late afternoon to the sound of bees in the orange blossoms. An idyll I was denied. Still, I could have chosen worse places to be exiled. It has been a struggle here but with hard work and careful planning I have made a go of it. Sent away as a disgraced leader and now, ten years later, once again I have shown them how to survive in a world where survival might not seem possible at first. But they are not here to see that.

Over the meal at night I fix him in my gaze, which he does not return. Again he eats hungrily, quickly. It reminds me of how we all used to be. We all ate quickly out of necessity. I remember him eating like that before. I watched him over a meal. He did not look up once, only when he had finished every last scrap. He even licked his fingers, which I found distasteful.

'Tomorrow you will come with me to the forest,' I say. 'You can help me bring back some wood.' I do not think he will be of much use but I'm sure by now he can walk properly and he has to start getting his strength back if he is to earn his keep.

In the morning after I've returned from the beach and we've finished breakfast I throw him the coat I found. He grabs it. I'm certain now it belonged to him. He fingers the cloth, the brass buttons, his lips open slightly as if in surprise. He looks like a boy. 'Put it on,' I say. 'It is yours, is it not? The coat of a General.' I do not put this as a question. He shows no reaction. Instead he removes my coat, stands up and puts the other on. It fits perfectly. He adjusts the collar and straightens his back. I watch with interest; he is like a soldier preparing for battle.

'Come.' I say, 'We're going to fetch wood,' and set off down the hill. He follows me but leaves a distance of around ten paces. He has recovered some of his strength but still shuffles along as if each step is a great effort. I listen to his steps in the mud, the soft sucking sound they make. Every time I stop to wait for him the noise stops too. He never approaches closer than the ten paces.

In the forest, without a word I throw him the bag I use for wood, which he catches, and I unhook the axe from my belt. He walks round me in a circle, watching me all the time. He comes to stand in front of me. He's on a little mound, the bag over his shoulder, his head held high, the coat like blood against his pale skin. As I chop down the tree and trim the branches he simply stands there, watching.

When I get out of breath I stop, bending over with my hands on my knees. I say, 'Your turn,' and hold out the axe. 'You can take over for a bit. I am tired.' I straighten up and walk towards him, holding out the axe, blade first. He drops the bag and shuffles away from me, holding up his arms slightly. His feet make furrows in the pine needles. I stop. 'What are you doing?' I am curt. 'What are you doing?' I repeat. 'Do you think I'm going to hurt you? Do you not think I would have done something by now if I was going to?' He says nothing. 'I rescued you, I have fed you, clothed you, why would I kill you now?' I have raised my voice. It sounds strange in the silence. I think I can hear an echo. I wave the axe in exasperation and turn back to the tree. He cowers, crouched down, his hands still over his head. Maybe I expect too much too soon.

The rain falls again now. I chop the tree into logs at a slow but steady pace. I can keep my breathing under control and still make good progress. Water drips from the end of my nose. I can also feel it running down my back. Steam rises from my body. The scent of wet pine chips fills the air. Andalus sits crouched under a tree, sheltering from the rain. He seems calmer now. In fact he might be asleep. From panic to sleep in a matter of minutes. I do not understand this person. I wish he would talk.

Andalus used to talk all the time. In fact I often wished he spoke less. We had different negotiating styles. He was all bluster, all promises, all camaraderie. This, however, overlay stubbornness and a determination to get his way. He came across as a fool but was far from it. He was a tough opponent and I came to respect him greatly. By the end of it, the time of the signing of the accord and the last official contact between the two groups, we formed something of a friendship. True, it was based on grudging respect on both sides and not on any deep emotional bond but by the end I began to know the man behind the talk, the man who, like me, cared deeply for his people, cared deeply enough to stop the war, at any cost.

There was a moment in which he let his guard down. He sat across the table from me, his head in his hands. Our aides had left the room. He did not move for ages. I thought he was asleep and was just about to get up from the table when he said to me, 'What have we done, Bran?' His voice was quivering. For a second I did not know what to say. 'At what price?' he went on. 'At what price does a thing become a luxury we should not have?'

'This is not a thing,' I said. 'This is not a luxury. This is peace.'

'We've ended the war, Bran, we have not brought peace. There will come a time when the world will not be able to forgive itself, or us. There will never be peace now.'

I said nothing. Instead I got up, went round to him, stood behind his left shoulder. His head was in his hands. I reached out my right hand and placed it on his shoulder. He gripped my hand. I felt his shoulder heave. I think he might have been crying. I could not tell. I was certain he was in turmoil though. I squeezed his shoulder, patted him on the back and said, 'We have done a good job, Andalus. We have fought for our people, for our interests. And now we have secured a future for them. Do not fear the future. Once we were enemies, once we were warriors. Now we are friends and statesmen. We have earned our sleep tonight.'

With that I left the room. It was a brief moment of intimacy but one that I appreciated. Several hours later we met for the celebratory dinner and he was again his jovial self, though he avoided eye contact with me.

I walk over to Andalus and prod him with my toe. He looks up sleepily. I give him a small bundle of wood to carry. He gets up and follows a few paces behind. Like a dog.

Later I collect some of the tubers and some grasses for a second bed, keeping their seeds to eat. I leave him in the cave when I do this. As I walk out I ask him to build up the fire. He gives no indication of having heard. I do not ask again.

In the grasslands I start to feel out of breath. My arms also ache from chopping down the tree. I sit down on a rock. Providing for two has taken it out of me and I am beginning to feel my age. Still a fit man but there is only so much one can do. One man, flesh and blood, set against the rising waters, the creep of the oceans, the clutch of the mud. If I look too far into the future it can be daunting. Nevertheless, that is what I must do. I keep track of the loss of the island so I will know exactly when the time is up so I can be awake, so I can stand facing the wall of water when it comes. So I can die proud. Now that I have to work more on collecting food and fuel I have less time to work on my map, on my calculations, my annotations. I used to know exactly when the time would be up but now I am less certain. It has only been a few days and this man is my responsibility but he is a burden. Duty was never a burden to me until now. There is nothing to say I have to take care of Andalus, nothing to stop me sending him on his way. Though since he has nowhere to go that would involve killing him. There is no one to judge here, nothing to stop me getting rid of my burden. Nothing but a sense of duty, not born out of any trivial sentiment – long ago we did away with that – but out of necessity. We were dutiful because we had to be, because that was how we survived. Survivors obeyed.

Duty is something I will never abandon. It carries me through, connecting my past with my future.

I have never planned a return to Bran. Surviving the voyage is not the issue. I have become adept at the tricks of survival. But I have been banished and respect that. It would be disrespectful of the laws I created. Andalus however, is a puzzle. What is the leader of the Axumite settlement doing in Bran territory? Either they have begun expanding or the old order has been overthrown. Mavericks may have taken over and begun to plan a resumption of the wars in an effort to win control of Bran and its resources. Though maybe he was simply sailing between islands and was blown off course in a freak storm. The stories can be made up in a number of ways. Whatever the stories though, the rules of the Programme have been broken and it should be my duty to report this. I need to try to find out more about him, more about why he is here. But it's impossible if he doesn't speak.

There is a myth in my land. One of the ancient gods – we no longer believe in gods – was banished by the council of the Heavens. His crime dissent. He sailed for weeks to the ends of the earth. When he finally found land he remained there for the rest of his days, hurling thunderbolts and storms at passing ships. When he died his petrified remains became a mountain on whose peak was engraved the visage of the god, serving as a warning, a curse, that all who gaze on it will too become stone in an unfamiliar land.

Another tells the story of a legendary king with the same name as mine. Fierce and always victorious in battle, at his death his countrymen cut off his head, drove a stake through it and placed it staring out to sea. Thus they cast a protective spell over the country against invading armies.

Myths are made of memories and memories are fallible but these two were pillars of Bran. Though we had no religion and little sentimentality, these stories, still told sometimes, are indicative of who we are as a people; both our sense of duty and respect and our pride and determination never to be defeated.

They mean a bit more than that to me though. I'm aware of some parallels. They speak of rejection and of veneration, of how easily things can turn. Two faces staring out to sea. One will avenge, the other protect.

Perhaps the presence of Andalus means that I, once more, have a duty to protect. His presence might mean I need to leave the island.

When I get back to the cave the fire has died out. Andalus is lying on the bed with his back to me. He turns around only when I give him food some time later. I call him General again. I ask him about Axum. But he does not look at me.

At first light I wake and look over and see Andalus has disappeared. I jump up.

Outside the cave a warm breeze is blowing and the clouds are thin. I cannot see him. I climb on top of the cave from where I can see more and scan the grasslands. But there is no sign of him. He cannot have gone far – in his shape no more than a mile or so. From the cave you cannot see the rocks where I fish and I think this is where he must be. I head off down the cliff path.

Walking slowly to the edge I peer over. He sits with his back towards me, facing out to sea. He is not fishing, just sitting. I watch him for a minute. His head begins to turn to the side slowly. It seems to turn too far to be natural. I crouch down, hiding. I do not make any sudden moves. I do not think he can see me but his head stays turned. Perhaps he is looking at something else, something further along the cliff, something behind me. I look around. I lie down in the grass and roll onto my back. A gull circles overhead.

Tora did not want to hear about the fighting. She knew what went on – everyone did – but she did not want to hear about life as a soldier, about things I had seen. Not about the killing and not about the buried relics of a forgotten age. I wanted to tell her but whenever I tried she turned away from me. If we were in bed she would roll away and lie on her side with her back to me. I would stop, turn to her and stroke her thigh. I did not berate her for not wanting to hear and eventually I stopped trying altogether. I suppose she needed distance from that. A gentler person I had never known and for her, I always thought, that she shared her bed with a man who had killed was distasteful. She did not resent my previous life, she did not blame me for it but I knew that she did not approve. Perhaps my attempts at stories of what past worlds might have been she associated with killing, or at least with dying.

If that was the case though, why did she allow herself to be involved with one whose job entailed what it did? It was a mystery to me. There were many things I found mysterious about her. Perhaps, though she did not approve, she could see the necessity of the Programme. No one really could approve, besides madmen, but we all knew it was necessary. This was another part of my life we did not talk about much. In spite of that she was a strength to me, someone I could count on, someone whose feelings and reactions I could predict and trust. I suppose she felt that if someone had to do it, it was better that it was me, a man devoted to the ideals of fairness and duty.

She would have struggled to find a man who had not killed. That was what we did, what we had to do. She was part of that forgotten world she didn't want to hear about, a throwback to a gentler age.

After a few minutes I get to my feet, return to the cave for my line and hooks and set off to join my companion. If I put a rod in his hands maybe he will take to fishing. It is not the right time of day but it is better than not fishing at all. I can sit him here every day and let him catch a few fish while I go about the rest of my work: gathering fuel, digging for tubers, harvesting seeds and furthering my survey. That could be the answer. I like fishing but if that is all he can do it will be better than nothing. It would free up more time to plan for the future.

He does not look around as I approach. I sit next to him, greet him, to which, as usual, he does not respond. I lift up his hands. I place the rod in them. He does not grip it. I stand up, taking it from him. 'Watch,' I say, and cast into the ocean. Again I try to make him take it. 'This is your job. If you want to eat, you will catch the food. That is the way it shall be.' Through this he watches me. Now though he turns his head away and stares out to sea. I raise my voice: 'I am not your keeper. I cannot provide for you as if you were my guest. You have to work if you want to stay here.' I try again and this time he grips the rod, though softly. I decide to leave him with it in the hope that he will try when I am not there. I head off for the peat beds. There is no time for my swim.

By the time I get back to the cave, lugging a sackful of peat, he has returned too. There is no fish and also, I notice, no fishing rod. I walk over to him and grab his arm. My fingers sink into his flesh as if it were a cushion. Between clenched teeth I say, 'I told you what would happen. From now on the only food you eat will be what you gather yourself.'

The rod is lying on the rocks where I left it. A small mercy. Though I can fashion another one quite easily, I am careful with the hooks. I brought a supply with me but they will eventually run out and I have not taught myself to fish with a spear. I will teach myself in a few years' time when I am down to my last hooks. I sit on the rocks waiting for a tug on the line.

I take the first fish I catch back with me to the cave. I also find a crab in one of the traps. I will eat well tonight.

Back in the cave I build up the fire. When it is ready I place the fish and the crab on a flat stone over the top of the fire. Andalus sits up on the bed and watches the food cooking. It is not long before I am ready to eat. I do so directly from the stone, picking up the flakes of fish with my fingers. The crab I move to one side and allow to cool. Andalus moves to the edge of the bed, looking expectantly at me. I stare back at him, chewing all the while. Eventually he drops his gaze and turns away from me. He lies on his side, facing the wall. I feel some guilt.

I say, not expecting a response, 'Tell me what happened.' He does not. 'Tell me, or starve.'

With my stomach full, leaning back against the cave and feeling warm for the first time in days, I try to explain Andalus's presence once again. I do not want a companion. Not one like this anyway. I do not like getting used to having a dependant. I think again of how he came to be here. If the Axumites have started exploring again, then the Brans need to know. No one would want a resumption of the hostilities. Perhaps Bran too has started exploring. We had no plans to do so when I left but that was then. Perhaps the world has changed. Or is about to.

And then I allow myself to think about what Andalus's presence requires. I think about going back.

3

The thought leaves a tightness in my stomach. I am like a man with a woman he loves, uncertain of how she feels, excited but too nervous to be happy. It does not surprise me that I have decided to go back almost without realising it.

I know too Andalus is an excuse, a reason I can use to explain my return. I am under no illusions. Going back will most likely mean either execution or at the very least imprisonment followed by banishment once again. Doing my duty and turning this man over will count for very little. I do not have unreasonable expectations but perhaps there will be time enough for me to tie up some loose ends, to see Tora and Abel once again, pick up some more supplies. I can leave a copy of my ten years' work behind with the authorities so they can study it and broaden, however slightly, the pool of knowledge. They should appreciate that. I will set to the work with renewed vigour when I return. I will have made my peace and leaving Andalus there would eliminate variables. A man is happiest when nothing is in doubt.

Ten years. It could be a lifetime, it could be all too brief. Ten years. Less time than Bran was at war, less time than I knew Tora, than I was

Marshal, than the time the Programme took to run its course. More time than it took us to end the war, to reduce the killing, the waste. More time than my trial, than it took to get here, than it took to say goodbye.

How many people have died in these ten years? The judge who sent me away? My assistants? Abel? Perhaps even, and the thought chills me, Tora herself. If she is not dead, it may be cruel to go back. Perhaps one day she awakes to a knocking on her door. It is me, wild-haired and exhausted after days at sea. I have come straight off the raft. 'Tora,' I say, though it is barely a croak and perhaps not even a word. Her eyes, blank at first, still full of sleep, suddenly come alive with recognition. What then? A smile? Tears? Does she throw herself at me or does she step back? Does a man appear on the stairs, a little girl down the passageway? Each and every thing is possible. Perhaps I will go back and find her flat boarded up, the neighbours behind locked doors peering round closed curtains.

He has not moved. He breathes lightly and rapidly. Asleep I presume, dreaming. I watch him, his bulk rising and falling. I count the days since he arrived. Three days short of two weeks. He appears to have lost no weight at all. Perhaps it takes longer. I think back to when I arrived but it is too long ago.

I wonder how he became like this. Did they have hierarchical rationing in Axum? Did they base one's food allowance on social rank? We would never have allowed that in Bran. The Programme was supposed to be carried out regardless of social position. If you were productive you were in no danger. Supposition though. I cannot get beyond his silence.

I have come across men struck dumb by the horrors of war. Some go quiet, some cannot stop talking. Each, given time, will more often than not come round. Time heals all manner of wounds.

I will need a few weeks to prepare for the journey. I must smoke as much fish as possible, harvest grains and tubers. Though we could catch fish on the way, ten years ago there were vast swathes of ocean that were lifeless (I am lucky on my island) and we could be sailing for days without catching anything. I will need to make a bigger raft. There are two of us now, after all. I can build a new mast and some oars. I can spend time rowing, which should cut the journey time down. But I must bank on three weeks still. I have a compass but it is still possible to go off course for a day or two. Also, though we will be rowing and will have a better sail, the raft will be heavier and will sit lower in the water. We will need fifty litres of water. It rains all the time but I do not want to be collecting rainwater in an unstable boat. Fifteen good-sized fish, a handful of grains and a tuber a day: that will be plenty and will allow me to be unconcerned about provisions on the way. I will have other thoughts to occupy me.

I boil water and add crushed seeds and grains to make gruel, which I eat with the remaining crab claw. Again I do not offer any to Andalus. I leave him in the cave when I go down to the beach for my morning swim.

While I swim I continue to think about the trip. The grains and tubers I can harvest a little at a time. They keep well. The fish that I smoke lasts three weeks before becoming inedible. Little is truly inedible but rotten fish is something I would rather avoid. If I take two weeks to prepare, the first fish will last a week into the voyage by which time it will long since have been eaten. A fish caught two days before I leave will last until almost the end of the voyage.

When I tell Andalus of my plans it may motivate him to work and to speak. Whether this would be out of fear or excitement I do not know. The two peoples are prohibited from entering the other's territory but if he has a reasonable excuse, after years of peace, it is doubtful whether he would be imprisoned. Perhaps even the prohibition has been repealed during this time. But if things have got worse, if the end of the Programme has caused tensions to rise again and supplies to dwindle, Andalus's presence here could very well be a pretext for a resumption of hostilities. And if he refuses to speak, he will be imprisoned for certain. I imagine him standing there silent in the face of the wrath of the settlement. It will not do. I will make him aware of this. I decide to refuse him food for a while longer. That too may loosen his tongue.

I return to the cave. Andalus stares at me, watching while I pick up my axe. I can feel his eyes on me but when I look at his face I see no hostility. The only emotion I have seen is fear. For the rest he is blank. A man with no voice and a man with no face.

I decide to tell him now of my plan to return. I sit close to him. I tilt my head to one side at first. I am still not going to tell him I know him. 'We are going away,' I begin. 'We are going to go on a trip in a raft I will build. I hope you will help.' His eyes meet mine. I stare into his pupils. 'We are going to a place called Bran. I used to be known there. I used to be known well. Bran will decide our fate. I hope it is to be a good one.' He drops his eyes from mine. I take his chin in my hand and lift it up. 'Will you help?' I ask. His mouth drops open. I think he is going to talk. He doesn't. Instead he gets to his feet and shuffles away from me, out the cave entrance. Where he was sitting I notice something, a piece of fish. Has he been secretly catching food while I've been out in the forest or at the peat beds? I feel anger. I shout after him, 'You will not plunder my island. You will not steal from me.' I get up and go over to the entrance. He is a long way down the hill and cannot hear me. He has moved surprisingly quickly.

I am not angry for long. My anger never lasts. I am too pleased to be going back to worry about Andalus overly much. But I will stick to my plan to try to make him talk. And I won't let him get away. He is essential to me now.

If I am to receive no help from Andalus I will need to make the most of my days. I will get up slightly earlier and forego the swim. I will alternate days of raft building with days of food collection and peat gathering. With fewer tasks in a day I can devote more time to each and accomplish more. It will be hard though and I will have little time for my survey.

It is dark today. As I set out for the forest, the clouds are so thick they shut out most of the light. It could be dusk. Though it is still dry near the cave, across the grasslands I see the rain fall in swathes, blown by the wind. Though it rarely rains heavily, today it will. It is not a good start to my labours.

I am right. The forest is wet underfoot. The rain seems to muffle any noise made by the breeze.

The first thing to do is to build the raft. I will need at least two trees for the base. The mast and oars can be made out of a third. By mid-afternoon I have felled three trees and stripped them of most of their branches. Once these are dry they will make a large bonfire. Or they will mean I can sit in a warm and completely dry cave for a few nights. But, unless I have miscalculated, they will not be sufficiently dry by the time I leave. They would give off too much smoke. I leave the trunks where they lie. Splitting them into planks can wait for the day after tomorrow.

In the cave I put some tubers in the fire. I am exhausted and do not go out again that day. I realise it might take me a little longer to adjust to a new, more vigorous routine. I spend the last hour of daylight making annotations. I write down the number of trees I have taken, the number remaining, the ages of the ones I have cut down. All the trees I have taken seem roughly the same age. As far as I can work out they're within a decade of each other at around fifty years old. I have three theories for this. The island experienced a few years of warmer weather when the saplings took root and now the lack of sun has stunted their growth. They are of a variety that only reaches sexual maturity at a great age, which would be why there are no saplings. They were sown by a previous castaway, a man armed only with seeds from some abandoned part of the world, seeds which gave birth to a barren progeny.

I have not given much thought to this – that the island was inhabited before me. Yet why not? It might rain constantly but enough light gets through for vegetation other than the trees to grow. There is peat. It is surrounded by ocean, which must once have been more bountiful than now. All in all it is not a bad place to live. I could have chosen a worse place to be a castaway. Perhaps there were people here first. The common age of the trees is a possible clue. There could be signs of previous humans all around, things that are there but that I cannot see. I could be living in the middle of a ruined city surrounded by ghostly chatter. We see what we want to see after all. But I am not convinced. I feel that I am the first one here, the first one to make his mark in this watery prison.

I do feel as if I am not alone though. The figures amidst the trees, heads peering over cliff tops, bodies merging into the black cliff walls. A consequence of being alone I tell myself. And of the life I have lived. The longer I have not been with others the more I imagine others, the more I feel I am being watched. Of course I am not alone now. Andalus, or Andalus's shadow, is with me. It is possible he follows me in such a way that I do not see him but I doubt it. He would not be able to hide from me, a man who has been living on this small island for a decade. He is too large to be stealthy and even if he weren't the island is mostly flat with little tall vegetation. Unless he was creeping through the mud on his belly I would be able to see him easily.

I do not feed him in the morning. Still he says nothing. I cannot, in good conscience, starve the man. Besides, I would not be able to return without him. My plan now is to feed him once a day at irregular times. I reason that if I can create uncertainty about whether he will or will not be fed he may be moved to question my actions. On a grander scale, this was why there was a war. Our uncertainty over whether there were enough resources for all led us to fight for our share. It led us to fight Andalus's people and it led to the Programme, which was, after all, a way to ensure there were never wars over food, land and water ever again, a way to ensure we knew what the future held. The Programme was put in place to prevent itself ever being necessary again, a contradiction my people lived with for many years.

I will not kill him but I will provoke him. It will be for his own good for he is unlikely to get much sympathy in the settlement if he cannot explain himself. That I treat him like an animal is not lost on me. Until he communicates with me that is the way I must be with him, for he can deserve no better.

I want him to talk to me before I reveal I know who he is. It is a good tactic to keep something hidden until the last moment. I have hinted that I know him of course. I wonder if it is this that is making him silent. If he were here on his own would he be talking? Speaking to everything: the plants, the birds, the rocks? It is me that puts the hand across his mouth stopping words. He could be the one playing the game. He recognises me and is searching for my weakness, gathering his strength for an attack, an attempt to take over this island.

It is unlikely I know. He seems completely in the dark about himself, about me. Again I think about what might have caused this. Driven away by a people turned against him he is no longer able to express himself, is no longer a man.

I will come clean with him before we leave. End the games.

I am stiff from yesterday's work. I feel it as I sit facing out to sea for seven hours. Bites are infrequent. I clutch my coat around me. My head nods. I am warm. All I can hear is the sea, the noise of the waves. I barely move other than once or twice to check the cliffs behind me.

I let my head slip forward till my chin lies on my chest. I feel my eyes closing. Then I jerk up suddenly, forcing air into my lungs. I feel as if I have stopped breathing. It is a few moments of panic. My line has stayed still in the oily water as if I hadn't moved. There is no room for error out here. A heart attack, a stroke and I will be left here on my own. Perhaps unable to move, waiting till the tide comes in and floats my body away. Andalus would be no help.

In the still of the late afternoon I return to the cave. Andalus is standing with his back to me in the middle of the cave. It appears he has not heard me coming. He sways slightly. I do not know if he is dancing or simply unsteady on his feet. He stumbles trying to turn around. Not dancing then. He stares at me. I break the gaze. 'Fish,' I say, holding out my catch. Is this what I have come to? Here stands a man with whom I once debated the future of our two settlements, the future of the known world. From a debate over the rights of men, the right to a secure future, the right to life, the duty to the lives of others; from this to a monosyllabic grunt spat out across a cave on an island no one remembers.

Andalus turns away and lies down once more. I do not feed him tonight. He lies on his back and I watch him in the gloom. He snores lightly.

The task of splitting a trunk into planks is an onerous one and requires skills I have not honed. Somehow though by the end of the day I have split two trunks into usable planks and chopped another tree down. My initial estimates of the amount of wood I will need have proved inaccurate. I will need two more trees. I am determined to build my boat better than the one that brought me here. I was lucky on the journey. Rough weather could easily have capsized the vessel. True, we do not get many storms anymore but they are not unheard of. That was what the settlement wanted. Lacking the courage, the conviction, to condemn me to death, they hoped nature would do their task for them. They should have remembered that nature has seldom done what we want. The crime for which I was banished was one born out of circumstances requiring an intervention in nature, a speeding up of its processes to avoid overwhelming it. That at least was how the Programme was billed and was the gist of my defence. Nature can support only so much life.

But I am being unfair to my people. They are not a violent, vindictive people in spite of what they went through. Pragmatic is a word that suits them, civilized and pragmatic.

It was an unusual court case. Not strictly fair. I was allowed a defence but I was condemned months before the trial began. I knew I would not walk out of there free. The numbers against the Programme had grown too rapidly. There was anger. I asked to send emissaries to our rivals to see what had happened there but this was refused. They may have suspected treachery. I wanted to ask my accusers how they could accuse me when it was their support that enabled me to carry out my duty. I wanted to point at them and say, 'You! You are in the dock too!' I wanted to shame them, to make them know their guilt, to tell them, taking their hands, 'See! You too have hands drenched in blood.' But I am not a melodramatic man and it would not have helped my cause. I understand that I was sacrificed for the sake of the greater good. Burnt at the stake while the crowds bayed around me. But there was nothing like that. It was an altogether quieter affair. Tora, sitting in the corner, barely glanced at me but supported me by coming to the trial every day and sitting through every minute of it. A few others came but not many. And they were mostly respectful. One man though had to be dragged from the court. Towards the end of the trial he started coming regularly and sitting in my eye line. I could feel him staring at me. One day in the middle of proceedings he got up and started screaming at me. He used language such that I never tolerated in the offices or from my acquaintances. Deplorable behaviour. I understand he lost several family members. During this episode Tora looked up at me. I fancy I could see tears in her eyes. But I could not see clearly. Guards were standing in front of me while their colleagues hauled the protester away kicking and screaming. I looked at Tora not at him, looked at her, trying to see more clearly, peering through a curtain of burly men.

The day has gone quickly. It has been one of my good days. I have worked hard and achieved much. It is a satisfying feeling. It is dusk when I turn to go. As I do I see Andalus. He is standing behind me about ten metres off. Just standing and looking at me. I do not know how long for. 'What are you doing?' I ask him. 'How long have you been there? What do you want?' He has startled me. I do not expect answers and I do not receive them. I walk towards him and he half turns as if letting me leave a room first. It is a gesture I remember him making years ago. He was always polite, there was no faulting him on that. This time though I cannot but feel a chill as I walk past.

I can hear him as he walks behind me back to the cave. It is a still day. In between the sucking noises made by my feet I hear his do the same. Only his are louder. When I stop his do too, momentarily behind mine. Like my shadow.

Later he takes his food without much show of eagerness or hunger. I finish before him and lie down. I am tired and fall asleep almost immediately.

The next day is to be spent collecting food. I return to the seashore and fish for several hours. I spend the afternoon harvesting grass seeds.

It is a good routine, one day of heavy labour, followed by one of foraging and peat gathering and it is one I stick to for another week by which time I have almost completed the raft and gathered about half the food we will need. The raft lies slightly below the high tide mark. I have made sure to drag the planks there from the forest. It is hard work but much easier than moving a whole raft from forest to sea. When I fish I can see it out of the corner of my eye, lashed to the rocks. When the tide was up I tested its balance and examined how low it sat in the water. The sight of the raft makes my heart beat a little faster. With every day the promised return to my land comes closer. I sometimes wonder why I have not attempted a return earlier but at heart I know I could not have done so.

The raft lacks a mast. I am determined to provide one. Not only will it allow me to complete the journey more quickly but it is a matter of pride. They will see I have lived well, that banishment has increased my ingenuity, my will to live, rather than diminishing it.

I am apprehensive about the reaction I will receive, though excited too. I want to return in triumph, a return that shows them I have prospered and that I bear them no grudge. But I am not foolish. I know I will have to approach warily, perhaps lie low for a few days until I am more certain of the mood of the country. Andalus though, might destroy that plan. It is difficult to hide one such as he, difficult to conceal his white bulk in the undergrowth. If there are still scouts in operation we will be picked up in no time. Two old men, one thin, one fat. Like some act from years ago: Andalus and Bran treading the boards.

Though I feed him little, my island companion does not grow thinner. I have not seen any more evidence of food that he might have gathered but I surmise he might be finding some somewhere. Also, he does not move much. For the weight to go he would have to exercise. It is now weeks since he washed up on shore. Weeks and he has not spoken a word, not communicated with me in any way. Sometimes he follows me around the island. I have seen him sitting on the rocks where I fish. But most of the time he appears to remain in the cave lying on the bed, staring at nothing. While I smoke the fish or carve an oar I watch him watching nothing.

The three days before my planned departure are agony. I cannot sleep and think only of the journey.

The mast is lashed into place. It is not strong enough for very high winds but we are unlikely to encounter those. I have already stored much of the food on the raft, wrapped in plastic to protect it from the rain and tied on securely. I have made one of the tarpaulins into a sail. It is makeshift but it will do.

Andalus seems to catch my agitation as well. During the night he gets up from the bed, opens the door and stands in the entrance to the cave, silhouetted against the night sky. He stands there for what seems like hours and then walks slowly back to bed. He does this for the final two nights. On the last evening I approach him after we have eaten. I have fed him well and prepared as much food as I could as we will be on rations now for three weeks. I take his face in my hands, squeezing so he feels pain and make him look at me. 'You. Andalus.' I say. 'Yes, I know who you are. I know you.' He continues to look straight at me. 'Do you understand what we are doing?' I have told him but I don't know how much he understands. 'We are going back to Bran. You remember Bran. You have been there years ago when you dealt with us. We fought a war, we made a peace. You and I. Andalus and Bran. You remember.' Silence. 'I am taking you there so they can send you back to where you come from. You cannot stay here. It is not allowed.' With this he pulls his face away, turns his head. I think he understands now.

I go and sit at the opposite end of the cave, my back to the wall, looking over at him sitting on the other side of the fire. 'Are you ready to tell me what happened? It has been four weeks since you arrived. I have done you no harm. What has happened to change you so much? You used to be the most talkative man I knew. I sometimes think we stopped fighting just so you would no longer have an excuse to keep on talking.' The joke gets no reaction.

I wait for a minute before proceeding. 'You will have to talk in Bran. We are not a vindictive people but you have broken a condition of the treaty. You know what the punishment is. We agreed on it in fact. You and I. They are sure to spare you if you can explain yourself: a mutiny, a rebellion, a banishment. I think that is what has happened to you. Banished, like me. But if you were you did not take enough care, were not lucky enough to avoid Bran territory. If you do not talk, if you do not explain yourself you might well be executed.' He says nothing.

He sits against the cave wall, his head slightly cocked. The fire flickers against his skin. Dies down. It grows darker in the cave.

'It's a rope we use. Death by hanging. It is easiest. There is no blood. Vomit, urine yes but no blood. It is quick too and with our limited resources, practical. You can reuse rope. We blindfold them of course. We are not dogs.'

He looks at me now but still says nothing. I think he looks at me. I cannot see his eyes.

'We blindfold them and tie their hands so they cannot move. We place the noose around their neck and there is a man whose job it is to kick away the stand when it is time. We do not allow people to watch. Just the hangman and one to make sure the victim does not escape. Then we bury the body. Just below the surface. Their faces have to be covered last. It is not a job people like doing, the burying of the dead.

'If you do not talk I fear that may happen to you. Perhaps they will launch a mission to Axum to seek an explanation but why would they bother? It will involve much expense and to what end? The remote possibility that their borders are under threat? The presence of one man, one bloated official, is unlikely to convince them of that.'

I realise I have raised my voice. I realise too that I might be right, that Bran might not care about this one man, that they might not see the potential significance. If they do not know who he is, if they do not recognise him – and I who knew him best took a while to do so – then he and I will encounter the same fate. Then there will be nothing to stop the hatred that has had ten years to fester. Ten years for the families of those put to death to foment revenge. I realise too there is no turning back. I have gone too far.

I stare at Andalus, willing a response. I sit there for hours, looking at him looking at me. It grows so dark he melts into the cave wall, becomes black, an outline. His eyes are sockets. If I half close mine he disappears altogether, disappears into the cave, into the rock, into the dirt. He is silent.

4

I have placed all the provisions and equipment on the raft already and lashed everything securely to the boards. I sit Andalus in the middle of the raft while I push it out to open water. When the water is up to my waist I climb on board. I row us out a few more metres, then hoist the sail. The wind is strong but I do not think it will be too strong for the mast. As the sail fills with the breeze I am exhilarated. We set off at a pace that belies the makeshift nature of the raft and its weight. We soon reach the end of my swimming range. The wind is coming from behind us, sweeping over the island. For a few seconds I close my eyes. I can feel the water surging beneath me, the wind and the spray.

I see Tora standing on the beach. She raises her head now. She is too far away for me to see her face.

There is a wake behind us, a stretch of calmer water leading back to the shore. I look back at the island and smile.

I feel something is wrong a second before it happens. The mast bends too far, a corner of the raft dips into the water and the opposite end lifts out. Andalus slips, the mast splits and falls forward. I seem not to hear it. I open my mouth to shout at Andalus but nothing escapes. He does not react. The mast falls across him and all I can see is his form draped in the sail, like a shroud, as I am flung overboard.

The water is warm, warmer than expected. I feel for a moment like going to sleep, like sinking to the bottom, to the golden sand, to be wrapped like a baby in fronds of seaweed. It is quiet here: no wind, no flapping sail, nothing.

Through the water I see Andalus in his white cloak. I see the shape of him, crouching forward in the bow, the edges breaking up, shimmering like a mirage.

Then I am on the surface coughing, spluttering. Jerking my head around the first thing I see is Andalus, having managed to shake free of the sail, standing on the raft looking over at me. The raft bobs on the waves. The mast lies broken across the bow. I swim over, grab hold of the raft and, still in the water, rest my head on the wet planks. I retch seawater, then close my eyes.

I hear him move. He holds a hand out to me. I look up at him but the sky is too bright to see clearly. I try to pull myself up but my grip on his arm slips. It is like he is not there. I wave him away.

The tide takes us in. When we reach the shore I lie down on the sand exhausted. Andalus also lies down, arms flung out above his head. The raft floats in the shallows. I do not move for hours. When I do it is to lash the raft to the rocks, take some food from it and head up towards the cave.

When I reach the cave I remember Andalus. I do not think him capable of sailing it but it would be a disaster if he were to try and take the raft on his own. I go back down and tap him on the shoulder. He gets to his feet without looking at me.

I know the broken mast is a mere setback and due to overzealousness on my part. It does not mean it can't be done and I am doomed to fail but it takes some time to realise this. I lie for two days in the cave, returning to the raft only to fetch provisions. I make two more marks on the wall. I make these marks very slowly.

On the third day I come to my senses. I fix the mast. It is a clean break and is repaired quite easily. I end up with a shorter, lighter mast, which is by no means a bad thing. I spend the fourth day foraging for tubers and grass seeds, determined to leave again on the fifth.

I leave Andalus in the cave all the while. He shows no signs of restlessness and spends most of the time sleeping. On the evening of the fourth day, examining my haul, I calculate that though I have made inroads into the provisions, which I cannot make up in one day, I still have enough for a nineteen or twenty-day voyage. It means I can leave for the second time five days after the first. I am excited once more.

The morning of the fifth day is quiet. There is a break in the rain. It is warm. When I reach the shoreline, Andalus following just behind me, I remember that I have not allowed for the changing time of the tides. We are almost four hours early. I could try to drag the raft down to where it will float but the sand is soft and it will take me a long time and cost me strength I may need later. I will have to wait. I sit on a rock but am restless. I remember how I used to feel before a battle: a tightness in the chest, rapid heartbeat, a tendency to be distracted. It is something you learn to control. You have to otherwise you would not last long. In the moments before battle you cannot lose focus. I have lost my edge. The long days of island time have hardened my body but dulled my instincts for a fight. True, I might have lost this before. I remember the first day of the trial. Tora was waiting with me. I could not sit still, was pacing around the room, not listening to what she was saying, trying instead to think of what I would say. She got to her feet once, came over to me. I held up my hand, impatiently, to stop her. She did stop. A little taken aback perhaps. I felt regret. But I was angry too. Angry with my people. Angry with her. She was no longer with me but was trying her best to be supportive. I stood behind her and kissed her head. Her shoulders shook a little. I did not hold her. It was my day, not hers. I get to my feet and set off down the beach at a rapid pace, almost running. I feel Andalus looking at me but I do not look back. He can do nothing while the tide is out.

I resolve to walk as far around the island as I can for half the time remaining then walk back. It is, I think, a way of saying goodbye. Since the arrival of my companion I have not had time to go on my explorations, my investigative walks. His arrival has increased the time I spend on essential tasks and decreased the time available for expanding knowledge of the island and its creatures. It is like that with people, the ones left over: too busy surviving to rebuild our knowledge. Except me. I was never too busy to try to piece together our story, to try to remember what we used to be. I feel resentful that I have been pushed into this mode by Andalus but it was with a higher purpose, that of my return, a return that will increase the store of knowledge and heal a bit more of the past.

But I make a detour first. Something I have sacrificed, besides my swims, besides my work, is my visits to the stone field. I go there now.

I have not been here but I have not stopped thinking about it, about what it means, about what it means to me. The rocks glisten. Many are half sunk in mud. I kneel down, rub the surface of one. It is smooth. I pick it up. A worm burrows into the soil where the stone lay.

Monuments are to honour the dead, to remember them. I try to picture the faces and I try to shut them out. It is no way to live. Like the bodies, the memories in shallow graves. I walk over them. My feet scuff the dirt from their faces.

I rub the mud off the stone. I take it back to the raft. It will return with me. A gesture, I know. Only a gesture.

I am saddened by what I see on my walk. Saddened for two reasons. With such a long break since my last time on this part of the island I can more easily notice the changes. Before, seeing the same piece of land once a week I would notice the water's creep in inches if at all. It was only by comparing it to my memory of where it had been weeks previously that I would really notice a difference. Week to week there was little to see. Now though, the change is stark. A large part of the cliff face has collapsed and water has seeped into new areas of grassland. Not seeing it for so long has made the pace of change appear more rapid. Yet I do not know, without doing calculations, which of three possibilities it is: whether it is only an appearance, an illusion caused by the change in gaps between observations, whether the pace really has accelerated, or even whether I made a mistake and the island is and always has been disappearing more quickly than it seemed. Though either the second or third possibility is troubling, I resolve not to let it bother me. I am, after all, leaving the island behind. Still, I do not like the uncertainty. I am not someone who tolerates uncertainty, unanswered questions.

The other reason I am saddened is a more sentimental one. Bleak though it is, it has been home and has nurtured me, held me to its wet bosom like a mother clinging to a child caught in a flood.

I see the rocks lying on the beach from some distance. They are like carcasses of a sea animal I saw once many years ago. Fifteen of them. I look round and can see more still embedded in the cliff walls. It is as if the island is starting to give up its treasure. A sparse treasure indeed.

They look like humans too, prostrate on the strand.

I run my fingers over the one that is paler than the others. It is slightly warm, warmer than expected. The ridges in it like skin.

There is something wrong with this scene, the bodies on the beach. I cannot put my finger on it. I leave it unsettled.

When I return, the tide is lapping at the raft and it is time to leave. I help Andalus on board, push the raft out further, climb on myself, hoist the sail and we are away again. This time there is no strong breeze and the sail is barely full. There are no surprises. We float away from the island like a couple of pleasure seekers, a pair of friends on an adventure for a day. I look back once. I see the beach, the cliffs in the north, my cave. The island is already grey, darker than the sky. From out here, it is a vast canvas of grey and in the centre, growing ever smaller, my life for the past decade, sinking into the sea, like a pebble dropped into a pool.

We drift for days like this. We eat, sleep, fish, drink. Sometimes I row. It is like life on the island before Andalus, having my routines back. The raft floats atop the shining sea. There is nothing else. No other vessel, no birds, no dolphins, no sound. I see the clouds reflected on the sea. Wrapping my coat around my head I hear my breathing, the water lapping against the wood, the occasional flap of the sail. Andalus sometimes snores. We sit at opposite ends of the raft. I am always hungry but not overly so. I am always thirsty too but again I can cope. I know how to ration myself. Andalus does not show dissent over the rationing. He does not show dissent at all. He lies with his hand in the water, the other across his brow. A feminine pose, the pose of a fop, a man of leisure. I wrap my coat around my head to block it out. The water, the raft, the man sitting opposite me, a silver fish, my wrinkled hands. I think of the going away and of the homecoming. My breathing grows louder in the dark.

She stands on the shoreline. One arm is at her side, the other to her forehead. She shades her eyes with her hand. The palm faces outwards, towards the sea. She watches me sail away. She is the only one who watches. I look at her too: the woman who loved but not enough.

I see her again there. Now she is older. Perhaps she is grey. She scans the sea with her hand held to her face. I wonder what is behind her, behind her on the plains, across the mountains, through the barren fields to the white walls of the settlement of Bran and the story of my future.

Days into the trip the sea becomes like glass. I think back to the ruined city, the statue at the bottom of the ocean. I wonder if I sail above it again. I look over the edge. I think of how it would be to drop silently down through the clear water, breathing water, swimming like a fish and then to stand on the streets of a long-forgotten settlement with buildings around me reaching up into the gloom. What would I find there? Around the corners of narrow streets, deep within abandoned buildings, would I find our story, our beginning? Deep in the murk shapes appear. We drift across them. Again I can see ruins floating beneath us. I look out for the statue, leaning over as far as I can. In the distance, too far to see properly, a shadow appears near the surface. I wonder if that is him. Still sleeping beneath the ocean. It flickers and is gone. We drift onwards.

Three days later we pick up some speed. I am hungry still. I too trail my fingers in the water. I try not to look at Andalus. Once he stood up. I screamed at him. I have not shouted like that for years. He cowered and I apologised. 'It's for your own good,' I told him. 'Just sit down. We'll be there in a few days.'

This was a guess. I have my compass to tell me the way to go but I do not know how far we have come. The only markers I have are ruined buildings at the bottom of the ocean. We could arrive tomorrow, we could arrive in a week. I think the pace is quicker overall than last time but the currents seem to be against us. Perhaps on the outward journey I caught one of them which bore me all the way to the island and now we are sailing against it, struggling against it. We point one way but the ocean moves the other beneath us, the island just over the horizon, waiting to suck me back in. Perhaps we have not moved at all.

But today I know this cannot be. Today I wake to sunshine. Before I even open my eyes I can feel it. I stand up and drink it in. I take off my shirt. I spread out my arms and lift up my face. I stand like this for what seems like hours. Standing on top of all this water, for the first time in ten years, I am dry. The boards of the raft begin to steam. Andalus lies unmoving.

Three days after the sun breaks through I see land.

5

It takes most of the day to reach the shore. About half-way through the day I begin to recognise the coastline and head for a small cove I remember.

It is a landscape vastly different from my island. There it is all water, sedge, mud, peat. Here it is all sunlight, red rock and gnarled trees most of which are barely taller than I am. The water in the cove is a deep blue. I can see the ocean floor metres below. There are shoals of fish and growths of seaweed on the white sand.

The cove is sheltered. The tides are not big here and I trust that the raft will be safe. I start to wonder whether I will need it again, wonder under what circumstances I might have to return here. I am used to being prepared though, which is why I keep it safe. I put thoughts of return to the back of my mind.

It is not the beach from which I set sail a decade ago. That is half a day's sail away down the coast. Once I recognised the coast I headed for this cove because it is further away from the settlement. I can take precautions to protect the raft from the elements but not from people. There were no people living here when I was Marshal but that was ten years ago. Any sign of habitation and I will move on and anchor even further up the coast. I do not want word of my arrival to reach the settlement before I do. I do not want them to have a chance to prepare a response before I have made my case. For the moment at least I must hide from curious glances, from prying eyes. Andalus will make it difficult. It is difficult to hide a fat white grub in a desert.

I step ashore. Something hits me when I do. I feel dry rock beneath my feet. I breathe in and taste dust, heat, a dry heat. It is only a smell, only a sense but my skin tingles. This air I breathe is home. As I tie the raft up I have a smile on my face.

Once the raft is secured I waste no time. I find a hollow amongst the rocks and lead Andalus to it. I tell him to wait in the shade. I tell him I will be gone for a little while looking for people. He is not to go anywhere, not to show his face, stick to the shadows. I have to lift his face to make him look at me. I cannot tell if he has understood but I leave him with some food and go.

I climb the cliff face. It is slow going. I am not used to the heat and the sun and I have been supine on a boat for three weeks with little food. My heart is pounding. There is a dryness at the back of my throat, something I have not felt for years. It is as if I am drying out. After being soaked in the peat waters of the island for years, all the water is now leaching out. I am a sponge left in the sun. Home or not, still a fish out of water.

At the top I sit and rest for a while. For miles there is nothing, no sign of habitation, no smoke trails, no cultivated fields. It is dry scrubland here: a few trees, dry grass, stunted bushes. In the distance are mountains, blue on the horizon. To the left and right the cliffs stretch as far as I can see. I was not expecting to see anyone but it is still a relief. I can breathe again.

I see an eagle. It swoops down to the plains and climbs again, clutching what seems to be a rabbit or a rat. Suddenly I feel my mouth watering. I have not eaten meat since my last meal in prison. The eagle's catch is evidence of meat. That is unusual. In some of the sparsely populated areas a few wild animals survived the famine and our relentless search for things with which to fill our stomachs but not many. And there were laws against unlicensed hunting. Anyone caught breaking the rules was subject to punishment. All adult members of the family had their rations suspended for two weeks. For some of the older people it was a death sentence.

It was a way of life that suited us and probably still suits the settlement. When life is threatened by its environment, there is little sense in antagonising it, little sense in testing a known breaking point. Rather rein in life than fight an omnipotent force. It was the thought behind the Programme, the set of rules of which no one wanted to speak but that saved us. Saved while killing.

I can almost smell the fire, the wood smoke. I can almost hear the crackling of dry branches and see the flames brighter than any on my island. The heat, the smell, the sound, those of a dry country free from the soaking waters of the island. I can smell the singed flesh of a rabbit. I know it was a rabbit the eagle had caught because I can see their burrows now. It will be risky to try to catch one of the rabbits. The last thing I want now is to be caught plundering the settlement's reserves. But I have to. We have another four days on foot and we have few provisions left.

Four days. The mountains I see in the distance are two days away and Bran lies another two days' march from the pass we will use to cross the range. Four days. It will seem like an eternity.

I can see no sign of humans around me and I can see for miles. If I am to catch food, this is a good place to do it. I return to the boat and to Andalus. He sits with his head down, his knees held to his chest. From the raft I take some twine and one of my crab nets. This will work equally well for a rabbit trap.

I think about making the journey at night, sleeping during the day, to avoid detection. I weigh up the pros and cons of doing so: more chance of slipping on the mountain, less chance of being detected. However, the only place to hide is on the mountain. If we slept during the day out here, under a tree or a bush, we could be seen for miles around. Best to be awake and hope that I see them first.

At night, under the stars, only momentarily do I feel ill at ease. Andalus and I eat well, feasting on rabbit meat and the fruits of a tree I remember from my youth. The unease is a feeling that it has been too easy so far. I did not have to wait long for the rabbits, they seemed to jump into the trap, and the only tree of its kind for miles around was laden with fruit. Just this must mean there are still no people in this area. They would not have left such abundance behind.

This part of the settlement's territories was never this fertile. Nowhere was. It is dry here but at the same time it is quite different to how I remember it. It is a fertile dryness. It has the look of a country anticipating spring. It clearly has enough water for grasses and trees and animals have returned. I wonder if all the world was like this once, or even more fertile. Streams running through meadows of sweet grass, their banks lined with fruit trees, fish making the water surge. Once we were many, I am certain of it, and if we were then surely other places were like this? I used to wonder, and the thought crosses my mind again, if we looked hard enough. Though as a people we spent years in wastelands searching for somewhere to live, did we settle too soon? Did we miss a land that knew no troubles, that had no unexplained ruins, that had a remembered past? A land filled with people, old and young, sick and healthy. Was it always around the next corner? But no. Everything I saw that pointed to a fantastical past was dead. Buried. Other clues to other worlds existed only in rumours and legends: stories of mythical creatures from a distant past, like the man encased in a mountain rock-face that was so meaningful for my people.

These thoughts do not occupy me for long. I have not seen stars like this for years. I have not seen them like this, seen them with this sense of wonder, since I was a boy. I would sometimes sleep under the stars when allowed, when there was no fighting, when there was no smoke, no dull-yellow fog hanging above our camp. I would lie under them and imagine myself visiting them, walking around the silver valleys with sand so soft it is like powder. I would imagine a land of perpetual night but a warm night, surrounded by even more stars, even more pinpricks of light. I would look at the moon, at its craters and wonder if anyone was looking down at me.

Tonight though, I find I am thinking of Tora and of the prospect of seeing her again. There are things that could prevent that. I make a list. One. I die in the next four days from heatstroke, an arrow from a scout, a poisoned animal. Two. When I reach the settlement they will not let me see her. Three. She is dead. I try to work out the odds of not seeing her. It proves too complicated.

I think back to our first meeting. It was beginning to be clear war was not succeeding, was depleting us of the sort of people we needed to overcome hardships, of young able-bodied men leaving instead the old and infirm, the women and children.

I was now directing the war from Bran, making occasional trips to the soldiers. At the time I was only beginning to formulate my campaign to become Marshal. We had a civilian ruler of sorts but I wanted to combine my role with his. I was planning the future of the settlement, laying out my vision for both Bran and Axum, the only two communities any of us had ever known.

At preliminary meetings with Andalus, my close colleagues, Abel included, and I had discussed the idea. We had to persuade the people to accept my plan. It became easier for both of us, Andalus and me, to move away from the military and into politics to achieve our aims. Our victory was made easier by the other's support since it was clear the idea would only work if both sides adopted it. And it was clear we would need strong leaders to see it through. I became Marshal of Bran. He kept his military title. We became leaders within a few months of each other.

It was several months, maybe even a year before this happened, that I was at a meeting held to debate the implications of the idea. Tora was sitting near the back of the hall. We were presenting our plans to prominent citizens and military officers. Tora was there I believe in her capacity as ration co-ordinator, a clerical post of some importance, reporting to a General.

I began by repeating the tenets of the Programme. There were to be three groups of people and three classes running across the groups. Administrators, producers and children under the age of thirteen would be classed A, B or C. Most citizens would be A-grade. Each class contained members of each group. Class was determined solely on the basis of whether a citizen was able to carry out his or her function, whether that was production or administration. Administrators such as myself and Tora would keep the settlement running smoothly and producers, such as Tora's mother, would farm or make goods for the use of the settlement. B-grade would be reserved for those with temporary incapacity, for those felt to be showing signs of dissent or of shirking responsibility, or for those felt to be not far off a C-grade because of age or infirmity. If a citizen could not or would not work, for whatever reason, he or she would no longer be of use, would be considered a burden and would be classed C. C-grade citizens would be eliminated.

The vulnerability in the grading system was that administrators would carry it out. I prevented that group hiding weaknesses in their family, friends or in themselves by instituting a system whereby everyone was regularly tested and examined by random members of the other groups. If anyone had concerns that another was in the wrong group they brought it to me. If anyone managed to beat the system it was never for very long.

I took it on myself to be the final arbitrator. I was the one who shifted names between A, B and C. I was the one to look them in their eyes. I took on a lot. I did sometimes wonder what would happen when my time came. Who would mark me? I did not dwell on that.

There would be no charity for those who couldn't work. The only charity was to be extended to healthy refugees and to the temporarily incapacitated.

The punishment for not reporting a potential downgrade to a C would be immediate reclassification for both parties as a C. Because of this I very rarely had to arbitrate. If someone fell seriously ill you did not hide it. You had a week to assess the severity of the illness. Some informed on members of their own family, unsurprisingly, as family members are usually the first to notice illness. Some people gave themselves up. Three of these were perfectly healthy but they refused to work. I had no choice. I did not understand their actions. Mostly though it was the old and infirm who gave themselves up, those who had had enough. They all died.

During the time of the Programme we experienced fifteen suicides. Some left notes naming me or my ideas. These were not included in our roster of the dead.

Citizens would also not be allowed to leave. Everything in the world was divided between Bran and Axum. There was so little in the world that we could not risk someone, not of the settlements, pilfering food that could nourish our brittle communities.

It was a very simple idea. The state of the world we found ourselves in and the years of wars had left just a few thousand people struggling to survive and those who could sustain us in years to come – the young – were dying every day. Due to lack of resources only those who could contribute would be allowed to be part of the two settlements, the two settlements that would build a new world.

It never struck me as a particularly original idea. Erase the weak for the sake of the strong. Sometimes the best ideas are so simple they feel as if they've been tried before. But it was an idea required for the times. It was our duty to ourselves to adopt it.

As I stopped talking Tora stood up. She was not supposed to speak. She had been invited to observe only, not being a leader of men. Some of the older men in the audience shouted at her, told her to hush. But she was not put off. I noticed her even as she began to rise and for a moment everything stopped for me. There was something in her, at the time I did not know what, that made other things seem unimportant. I did not hear much of what she said, or do not remember. I do remember her voice though. It was soft, yet clear and firm. Somehow it held out through the cat calls, through the disapproval of men who had killed for her and for others like her. She was not to be swayed. Rather die hungry than be tainted by the murder of your own people, was one of her lines that I do remember. She was a little emotive that day but I think she came across well, certainly as determined and courageous. As she was being led away she looked back at me. It was the first time she did that. She looked back and met my eyes for what seemed like a minute but was probably just a second.

That was, I believe, the strongest opposition I encountered to the idea. That, and the screams of the victims and their families.

We did not call them victims. We called them martyrs. A word from another time. One who believes in sacrifice and sacrifices himself to save others.

A week later I chanced upon her in the street. I was walking one way on one side of the street, she was walking the other way on the other side. She saw me too. I actually held up my hand to wave without realising it. She seemed to begin to respond and then thought better of it. It was a year later when finally I kissed her. A year later when she came round to the idea. At least, came round enough not to fight anymore.

I think of Tora and listen to the crickets – a sound I haven't heard for years. It takes a long time to fall asleep.

When I wake I check that the raft is secure. I leave most of the equipment tied down on it. I take only some twine, my knife, my notes and a container for water. I don't want to be weighed down. I take the stone too. It is one of the smaller ones but this is weight enough.

I tap Andalus on the shoulder. He stands up straight away, takes the food I give him and sets off in exactly the right direction, walking and eating at the same time. I forget that he too knows this country. I follow a few paces behind.

He cannot keep it up though and after an hour or two we have resumed our normal position of me in front, turning round every hundred paces or so waiting for him to catch up.

The next day in the early morning the mountains ahead of us catch the sun. I can see a green valley leading up to the summit of one of the mountains. This is the pass. In this light everything is clear. I feel I can touch the mountain, though it is yet miles away. I breathe the cold dry air. I can also feel the heat of the sun beginning to warm the landscape, as if I were a rock basking in the rays, as if I were the grass, the leaves, singing in the wind.

This pass is the only way across the mountains. I have to hope that we don't meet anyone coming the other way.

I have been scanning the horizon for people all the time. My eyesight is still keen and I have not seen anyone. I wonder though. I wonder if we have been seen already and the watchers take care to remain out of sight. Last night I pictured them just beyond the circle of light made by the campfire. They watched expressionless as we ate and slept.

We walk through the day watching the mountains grow ever larger. We make camp at the base of the pass. We eat well again that night and lie down under the stars. The country we are in has changed so much in ten years. What else will have changed? I think of my reception.

Will I get a chance to say what I want, to tell them why I'm here, why I'm back, before a knife in my back stops my tongue, before an arrow pierces my throat?

I take a branch from the fire and walk around our camp. I hold the branch above my head. It illuminates bushes, sand, trees, but no people. I extinguish it and stand for a while in the cool air. I am in complete darkness watching Andalus through the fire. Just his head appears through the flames and the smoke. Slowly my eyes grow accustomed to the dark. The night opens before me.

It is further to the summit than it seems. At mid-morning we leave the trees behind and walk, following the natural contours of the slope, criss-crossing the side of it. The way up is defined by a sheer drop to our left and by scree to our right. The sight of the peak brings energy surging to my legs. Within minutes though, my lungs are bursting and I can think of nothing but where to place my feet and how to slow my breathing. I stop, realising Andalus has disappeared. I shiver as a breeze comes over the peak. I stare down the path, close my eyes, open them. I see him again. He is struggling. I wait.

I should not push him too hard. If he were to die, to disappear, I would have no excuse. I wait till his breathing has slowed then offer him some water. He drinks the whole thing in one go. I do not stop him. I say gently, 'We will go more slowly. You are not made for this. I would not want you to die before we reach the settlement.' He looks at me when I say that. He appears to have half a smile, as if he suspects the double meaning of my words. It is an expression I remember from earlier days.

It is afternoon by the time we reach the summit. We round an outcrop and there it is. A vast plain stretches away beneath us. It is coloured variously, yellow, pink, blue, white, as far as I can see. Wildflowers softening the landscape, giving the air, it seems, a delicate perfume. I am amazed. I have never seen flowers like this. But the flowers are not all I can see. There in the distance, so far away you cannot focus directly on it is a plume of smoke and a smudge on the horizon. This is it. This is the settlement I left all those years ago. I stare at it for ages. Andalus comes up and I can sense him watching me. I turn to him briefly and point to the smudge. He looks blankly at it and goes to sit on a rock.

I am surprised we have not come across any people. Though we are still probably two days' march away, I would expect there to be scouts, patrols. I would expect farmers and foragers. I would expect to see signs of nomads, the people who choose not to live within the security of the settlement, though these could have been eliminated in the intervening years. Even in my day there were not many left. Yet we have seen nothing. Nothing and no one. I wonder again if they have seen us. Perhaps they have been camping at the top of this mountain, waiting, looking out at the two figures approaching slowly across the plain. Perhaps now they are hiding behind the next rock, waiting to fall on us.

We descend to the valley floor where we make camp. I sleep little in the warm night. I fancy I can smell the people. Wood smoke, charred meat, sewers, the smell of water seeping through sunbaked earth in sluices that I helped dig. I fancy too I can hear them: voices, breathing, laughter even. It is like I'm back on the island.

The next day we walk towards the point on the horizon where I saw the settlement. We walk through fields of flowers.

But this is not paradise. This is what we fought over, lands like this. We fought and buried our dead under the ground of fields like these. Face upward, naked and open to the earth. Perhaps we thought this was a way of bringing the earth back. There are rumours we were worshippers of nature once. Perhaps the earth is in our blood after all, our veins running with soil like an hourglass.

Towards dusk a solitary tree appears on the horizon. We have left the flowers behind now and this part of the plain is white. Little grows in the rocky soil. The tree is a stark blot on the landscape. When we get closer I can see that it is dead. It is large and still sturdy but dead. I remember this tree. It was not dead then. On one of the very few occasions that we saw each other outside of our normal hours Tora and I came here. We sat in the shade. We didn't talk much. She lay with her head in my lap. I stroked her hair. I reach out and touch the bark. It is smooth, like paper. I remember the touch of her hair.

We spend the night camped beneath the tree. It is four hours from here to the town walls.

We start early in the morning and soon crops begin to appear: fields of barley, wheat and finally corn that is taller than I am. We have no choice but to walk through it.

It is quieter and darker in the field of corn. We walk for several minutes before I see it. Or think I see it. Between the leaves, hidden by shadows, a face. A momentary glimpse of a face and a swish of the corn leaves. I stop, chilled. I hold out my hand to Andalus but he has stopped already. I wait. There is only stillness. I walk forward a metre. Stop. Listen. Again nothing. There is nothing I can do about it anyway. If I am to be discovered now then so be it. I walk on.

A while later without warning, we burst through the last of the maize. In front of us is a white road curving around the field and on the other side is an orchard of orange trees. Under the trees is long grass. It looks soft and is such a luminescent green I imagine the water here must be abundant. I think back to Tora's mother dozing in the speckled shade beneath her orange tree, protecting what little fruit it managed to bear. These trees bear no relation to their parents. They are laden with green leaves and ripening fruit.

But beyond the orchard is what we have come for. The timber walls of the town rise above the trees. The walls, baked grey by the sun, are tall enough to prevent us seeing any buildings or roofs. Except one, and this one I know. This one is so familiar as to have been anchored in my mind. My offices – the offices of the Marshal of Bran. I feel my heart beating. I pull Andalus across the road and into the shade of the trees. The walls disappear again.

I sit for a few moments thinking but there is no planning to be done now, no calculations. All that remains is to walk around the walls to the gate, straight down the main thoroughfare and up to the office. There I will find an official, whether that be Marshal Abel or someone else, and say what I plan to, say something: 'Here I am. Kill your Marshal if you must,' and that will be that. That is the extent of it. What happens after that needs no planning. It needs adaptation to circumstance.

I rise, helping Andalus to his feet and begin the walk. We are on the side of the town exactly opposite the gates. I walk anti-clockwise, making sure Andalus does not stray. I walk within sight of the road, though far enough into the trees to make sure we can hide quickly. When we have done half the circuit of the walls, I see the road branch to the left, leading to the gates. I follow it, still in the orchard, until I judge we are about thirty metres from the walls, take a deep breath, and head out into the sunlight. I am holding Andalus by the hand. From here we need to walk quickly but not too quickly, and confidently but without arrogance.

We emerge onto the road and I notice the gates are shut. I don't stop however as they are often shut. I scan the turrets above the gate for sentries but there is no one there, no one that I can see. This is different. I walk up to the gates. I am unsure what to do. Hesitating at first, I knock. There is no reply. I knock again, louder this time. I wait. I put my ear to the door but cannot hear a thing. I open my hand and bang on the door three times. I look round at Andalus. He has his back to me. He is rocking on his heels, facing the plains, facing the mountains. He begins to walk away. I grab him by the arm, tell him to stop.

I turn back to the gates. There is no handle on the outside. Instead I push. I put my shoulder to the gate and shove but nothing gives. I call out, 'Bran.' I call again, 'Bran.' I think I can hear an echo. I put my ear to the gate but I can hear no footsteps. It is mid-afternoon.

I take a step back, grab Andalus's arm again and walk away. I walk all around the town looking for someone to let us in, someone who can tell me where everyone is.

But I see no one. Sometimes Andalus walks ahead of me. I watch him. He appears to melt into the earth. There is a heat mirage. His feet disappear. He floats, circling the town.

We are back at the gates. I try again – knocking, calling – but there is no answer. I sit down, my back against one of the gates, my head resting against the wood. I pull Andalus down beside me. I close my eyes and wait.

I listen. I find myself listening for waves, for wind, for gulls. There are none of these. Thoughts float to the surface. I try to listen for other things to quieten them.

Eventually I fall asleep.

6

I wake with a start. It is an hour after sunrise. I look around. Andalus is slumped against the wall a little way off. To my left I notice that now one of the gates is ajar. Only fractionally but open nonetheless. I did not hear this during the night, did not feel anyone creep past. I am surprised. I am usually a light sleeper.

I push it further open. The street opens before me. Shadows of the rooftops stretch across the dust in the street. I look down. There are footprints in the dust. The houses on one side in the shade are dark, the others bright, lit by the sun. All are grey. Old wood, weathered by years of sun, rain, wind and the occasional snowstorm. There is no one in the street.

I push the gate open and turn to call Andalus but he is right behind me, also looking into the town. I take him by the arm and we walk through the gates into the settlement of Bran.

I look to the right and left of me. The houses stand silent. My people have turned into late risers. The windows that have curtains have them drawn. Those that don't are black. I see no one in the houses.

But I sense people. As I got used to speaking, perhaps so I have to get used to seeing people again. I sense them around me in their multitudes. If I reach out an arm suddenly I could touch one. They shift as I move down the street to avoid knocking me, a parting ocean. They surround me, staring. I feel their breath on my neck. I cannot see them. When I pass they stare at my back.

And then I do see someone. She stands at the end of the street. A girl. She has her hands at her sides and is looking at the ground. She wears a red coat. Something about her startles me. I call out to her, 'Hello.' When she doesn't answer I call again. She does not look up. The second time she turns around and runs off, disappearing round a corner. I let her go. Again the streets are deserted.

I walk in the same direction. As I turn the corner I see it straight ahead, the complex housing the settlement's administrative buildings. The buildings grow taller as we approach. Two and three-storey wooden structures, which, though they look fragile, have withstood many a year. I can see that the gate to the complex is open.

My pace is quicker now. I have once more taken hold of Andalus and we march straight up to the gate and through it. We are in the courtyard. Around it are doors leading to various chambers, various places of appeal, boards, licensing departments. The doors have the same white plaques I remember but the yard is empty. Usually there are scores of people here on some or other business but nothing now. It is empty and every door is closed. I look around, letting go of Andalus's arm.

It is not what I was expecting. It is early in the morning but the settlement wakes early and the hub of Bran can never afford to close down. I go up to the first door. The sign says Ministry of Agriculture. I smile. It was me who insisted we give these departments grand names. They conveyed a sense of purpose. The only truly important office in this building was my own. That was where all the major decisions were made. Though it was called the Ministry of Agriculture, all that happened there was the counting of the crops we managed to grow and the monitoring of our small livestock herds. Next door the Farming Licensing Agency did not license farms or regulate the bigger providers. Instead it handed out licences to individual citizens to grow certain crops for public consumption on small areas of land. Though this was all it did, it was important, for a licence was, for many, the difference between an A or B citizen's grade and a C. There were often queues of supplicants outside its doors, mostly old women, a few old men. I remember standing in my offices, leaning out the window, looking down on these people. I saw Tora's mother in the crowd. I sent down word that she was to be licensed. It was a reprieve, though inevitably not one that lasted forever. Like the Ministry of Agriculture the Farming Licensing Agency is closed.

The death of Tora's mother was not a simple affair, not as simple as I may have intimated. She was well liked in our town. There was a silence, a darkening, when it became known what had happened to her. I had to walk to her home. I went unaccompanied and let myself in. I did this because I had taken on the task of deciding who would be classified C. I did this to spare others the task. It was not a pleasant thing and I do not lack compassion. I let myself in and went to her in her bed. Her eyes were closed. I brushed my fingers over her cheek. The skin of old people can feel lifeless, like dry sand. Hers was cold too. An eye fluttered open. She looked at me with the one eye. It was open wide. She did not blink at all. I looked into it and waved my hand in front of her. She reached up to me with one arm. She seemed to be trying to move her mouth. Sound came out but it was nothing. Not a word. A gurgle. It was fear. Fear of me, the bringer of death.

I knew she was paralysed on one side of her body. The rules were clear. She would have to hang.

I sent a cart for her. Or rather I went with it. Just me and the hangman. There was no need for a soldier this time as there was no chance she'd be able to escape. I went with all of them. I wanted them all to see compassion before they died, to see that their hanging would not be in vain. It was my responsibility.

I lifted her from the bed. She was remarkably heavy. The tongue moving, gurgling again. The one eye open, her good arm and leg thrashing. I placed her in the cart and led her out through the town gates. It was after sunset but there was a full moon. The hangman drew the cart after him. There was a loud crack and the cart began to tip over. An axle had snapped. I ran to it but was too late. It landed on its side and she slid out. The blanket fell off her and her legs were uncovered. I saw the veins and the bruises in the moonlight. The body of an old woman. I lifted her to a sitting position. Her head lolled to one side and I took it in my hands. She was breathing quickly now. I felt a warm liquid on my hand. Her face was cut from the fall and bleeding heavily. So much blood from someone half dead. I wiped my hand in the dirt. I lifted her up, placed her over my shoulder. Through my clothes I felt her, I felt her heart beat. A broken woman but a heartbeat so powerful I could feel it through my coat.

On the way she vomited. I was covered in it. I felt myself gag. But I did not allow myself to let go. I carried her to the trees and set her down. 'Do it,' I said to the hangman. He did not move. I went up to him and slapped him across the face with the back of my hand. 'This is your duty,' I said to him. 'This is what you contribute.'

From behind me I heard a whimpering. I knelt in front of her. I wiped the sick from her mouth, the blood from her face. I wanted to say something to her. I wanted to whisper something to her so that the hangman wouldn't hear. I wanted to whisper something that would make her unafraid, that would make her understand, that would make her not see me there in front of her preparing her for death. I had something ready to say but I couldn't say it. I cannot remember what it was. I couldn't say it. I had to hold her up. Her legs wouldn't support her. I held her up from behind while the noose was tightened around her neck. It was like she was already dead but I could feel her shaking. I held her tight, smelling her warm, old woman smell, then I let her go.

I can remember feeling grateful that Tora was not there, that she would never have to witness something like this.

When the act was done we released the body from the noose. We placed her in a sack. There were two bodies already in bags from the day before. They were to be buried the next morning. I did not see where she was buried.

Back in my office I stood at the window in the moonlight. I was naked. I had a damp cloth and wiped myself. I slowly wiped away the blood and the vomit. I stood there for an hour, cleaning myself.

I step back and look up at the windows for the first time since entering the courtyard. There, though I cannot be certain, I see a shadow, a figure slipping quickly back into the dark and out of sight. I stare up for a minute but I can see nothing more. It was no more than a flash.

I look round at Andalus. He stands in the middle of the courtyard. His pose mirrors that of the girl, hands at his side, head down, red coat.

I continue round the circle of doors. Each is looking older. If the paint is not peeling then the plaque is obscured, but the complex still appears to be in use as the settlement's administrative offices. Why leave the names in place if not?

Two-thirds of the way round I come to my door, the entrance to my offices. I think I deliberately started on the far end, deliberately did not come to this door first. I wonder who will answer the door and who is Marshal. Will it still be Abel or would he have been replaced? It has been only a decade though and he was a young man with ascetic habits. Unless he has died it will probably still be him. I wonder what his reaction will be.

Though it might seem strange, I did not, and do not resent him for going behind my back. We were both politicians and he was the quicker at sensing the change in sentiment. He sought to encourage it, while I attempted to change it. He had the arguments that appealed though. No doubt he had the easier path but I knew what I was doing. I believed in what I was doing and I respected his belief too. Perhaps that made it difficult for him to shake hands with me when I left. Perhaps there is nothing more powerful than a man who admits defeat graciously. It is not a power of this world though.

I shook his hand on the grey beach and his hand was wet and he would not look me in the eyes. Alongside him was Tora. Her hair flicked in the salty breeze.

Sometimes, I admit, I did not quite know what to make of Abel. Though he was my second-in-command, he was difficult to read. Sometimes he appeared displeased when, probably, he was just being efficient.

I wonder what would have happened had I chosen someone else to be my successor. I have often wondered this.

This door at least is well kept. It gleams white and the plaque, this one made of brass, has been recently polished. It simply reads 'Marshal'.

I lift my hand to knock but the door opens immediately, as if someone was waiting for me. The man standing before me is dressed in the same uniform I used to wear and has medals pinned to his chest. He is about my age and grey. He looks at me. It is not Abel. I don't know whether I am disappointed or not.

All the same he looks familiar. Perhaps it is just the uniform but I think he may have been one of my generals in the wars. I cannot place him immediately though. He says nothing, merely stands in the doorway with a blank expression, looking, unblinking, at me.

'Good morning,' I say.

Though not immediately, the man inclines his head in greeting.

I have been thinking of this moment for a long time, longer perhaps than I realise. I have planned it, planned what to say but the person I was talking to was Abel, not this man before me.

'I am looking for the Marshal,' I say. 'Are you him?'

The man nods his head. 'I am Marshal Jura.' I feel disappointment but something else as well. I cannot put my finger on it.

'I am …' I begin, then stop. 'I have brought this man here. I have brought him to you for your attention.'

The Marshal's stare follows the direction of my gesture. 'Yes?' he asks. He is not rude but it is clear he wants me to get to the point and clear he does not immediately recognise either me or Andalus.

'His name is General Andalus,' I say. I watch closely for a reaction. There is none. His eyes don't blink.

'He was once, perhaps still is, General of Axum. I found him within our limits. I have tried to interrogate him to find out his purpose but he has not spoken. Though I do not believe his intentions are hostile, he is nevertheless an alien and in breach of the peace agreement. Not only that but as it is Andalus himself, his presence outside Axum and in Bran is a worrying sign.'

I wait for the Marshal to say something. But he doesn't. His face is impassive. He simply looks straight at me. I wonder briefly if he is consciously trying to appear as blank as possible.

'He is a sign we must attempt to explain. His appearance is of great concern to me. If there has been a mutiny, we need to know. If, like here, there has been a peaceful regime change,' I pause for effect but he gives no sign of noticing the irony, 'then we need to know that as well. I have brought him here as befits my duty as a loyal subject of Bran.'

'Andalus.' It is not a question, simply a statement of the name.

'Yes, Andalus.' I stare back at him. There is a long pause and the Marshal breaks it first.

'You have brought him?'

I wave my hand behind me without turning around and nod my head. 'I have.'

He looks over my shoulder for what seems like a long time, then back at me, and says,

'I see no one.'

I turn around this time and gesture towards Andalus who has moved off to the entrance to the courtyard. 'Him,' I say impatiently. 'That man standing with his back to us.'

The Marshal looks towards the entrance, then at me. He pauses for some time. Finally he says, 'You must go home, old man. We are due for rain.'

With that he steps back inside and makes to close the door. I am momentarily caught off-guard but I step forward before he can close it completely. I place my hand on the door and put my foot over the threshold. I am taller than he is. I speak slowly, evenly. 'You do know who I am, don't you?'

He pulls back from me. His expression changes, very briefly, to one of anger. He does not answer my question. Instead he simply says, 'Go.'

'I must speak to you about this man, about what he means.' I still push against the door.

The Marshal looks to one side as if another was standing there out of sight. He seems to nod. After a slight pause he says, 'Tomorrow.' With that he moves my hand and closes the door. He does not do it in an irritable way. It is quite gentle in fact. All the same, I am annoyed at the lack of concern shown by the Marshal.

I stand staring at the door for a minute before banging on it with my fist. It does not open.

I have no option but to leave and return at the appointed time. If the Marshal will not see me now I will find Tora and perhaps Abel first. I fetch Andalus, who has wandered towards the first set of doors, and lead him out of the courtyard.

I see people outside. A man and a woman stand staring at the entrance to the courtyard, as if waiting for someone to come out. When they see me they turn away. They begin talking to each other.

There are others in the street too now. Not many and most are children. They run after each other kicking up dust that then seems to hang in the air. I look around for the girl I saw before but she is nowhere to be seen. Amongst the adults there is no one I remember. No one looks at me.

This is not what I expected at all. Not recognised in the street, not recognised by the new Marshal, who registered no surprise or concern at the news of Andalus. No second glances. I have not been accosted or arrested. I have not planned for this.

The people start hurrying, almost running. Perhaps because I am so used to it on my island I do not notice immediately that it has begun to rain. I lift up my face to the rain and can feel drops begin to wash the dust from my skin. I feel something. I want to call it homesickness but it cannot be.

Once more I have the streets to myself. To myself and Andalus. I take him by the arm again and lead him deeper into the town. The rain makes it dark, stains the wood, turns the dust from white to brown. I sniff the smell of baked earth released by the rain. I walk slowly past house after house. For some I can remember who lives, or lived, there. For others I cannot. I walk through a warren of streets. It is all so familiar but changed as well. All so long ago. There are some new buildings but only a few. Though the earth beyond the gates appears more fertile than before, within the walls the town still appears barren. There are few plants, little colour. Here and there a door is painted red, yellow, green but little else.

I walk past the patch of ground where Tora's mother had her garden. The chair where she used to sit is gone. The orange tree is still there. In contrast to its surrounds, it is lush. I stop and stand under it. I feel the drops washed off its leaves land on my skin.

I have spent the greater part of my life walking these streets, smelling the rain, the wood, the dust, listening to the chatter of neighbours in the streets. It is all the same, the buildings rising sometimes to three or four storeys, raised wooden porches, stairways on the outside, balconies. Each structure a masterpiece of engineering. Nothing special to look at, seemingly flimsy and ramshackle but actually sturdy and each building a warren of flats and rooms. They are built close together, initially to provide a sense of security. The settlement grew from a few buildings huddled together as if for warmth into a sizeable town. But even in later years, when there was less need for security, when the town was well fortified and the wars were over, we carried on building in the same manner. It was a comfort, I suppose, in times of hardship.

As well as being the town's Marshal, I was also its historian. I drew maps of its beginnings, of the positions of the first houses. I talked to the founding fathers before they died. I nailed a plaque to the door of the oldest building, another to the door of the first clinic, another to the building on the site of the first barn. I was, truly, the man who knew this town the best, who, I dare say, still knows it best.

The settlement and the island. Maps, notes, beginnings. My work here mirrored by my work on the island. Though, it is true, here it was with a greater sense of permanence.

Sometimes it is the things you know best that seem to change the most. Because you know them the best, in fact. You notice changes in your body – wrinkles, grey hair – before you note them on a lover's, before you note them on a friend's. This building with an extension, that with a new porch, another with different coloured curtains, yet another that used to be a ministerial house and is now an alms house. That in itself a big difference.

Sometimes, admittedly, it is in the things you know best that you are the last to notice change. If I had had the signs pointed out to me earlier – the turning of a shoulder, the hush when I walked into a room, the hardening of smiles – perhaps I would have lasted longer. Perhaps not a great politician after all.

Yet, would I have done things differently? Indeed, could I have done things differently? The townspeople, like dogs, followed my commands faithfully. Like curs they followed me because I led, because I showed them the way. I showed them how to live, how to survive. They came from everywhere and nowhere with nothing to live for, until they found someone to lead them out of the darkness and into a brave new world. Because I showed them how to live they did not mind killing for me, because it was not killing for me, it was for them. And they were not stupid. Each and every one knew what he was doing. It was I who was stupid. I had not reckoned with the luxury of guilt. Once survival is ensured, guilt sets in. Only once survival is ensured can guilt set in. And guilt motivates change. My fault. Not a very good politician at all.

Still, I love this town, these people. They have been my life too. I bear them no grudge.

The rain does not last for long. The sun comes out again. Steam begins to rise from the tops of the houses.

I breathe deeply. It has been a strange reception, perhaps even a slight setback but I am home and I am not hanging from the end of a rope. I put my arm around Andalus and squeeze his shoulders. He looks surprised.

I am hungry, not having eaten since a couple of oranges last night. I decide to try to find the old kitchens. I have no card or ration allocation and will have to gamble on the compassion of the cook. There is an additional reason for going to the kitchens of course. I hope to find Tora there.

As I walk the streets, I find myself scanning faces, searching for one familiar, searching for the brown curls hanging to her shoulders, the slim waist, the purposeful stride. I believe I would know her even if I could not see her face, even if, as in some children's story, she has grown faceless. She is ingrained in me. I try to picture her face but I cannot. I could remember her on the island but here, where I am closer, it has gone. Her face was as familiar as my own but that too I cannot picture clearly, having not seen it in anything other than a pool of water for ten years. But I know her walk, the gait, the way of tossing her head so the curls would not hang over her eyes. I remember the eyes too, if not her whole face. I remember the smile. Her smile. It was never complete, never completely joyous but it had a power over me. I kept looking for it all those years I was with her, kept looking for the creases at the corner of her mouth, the one dimple, the shy look away from me when she did smile. All that I can remember but not her face.

Her smile was an obsession for me. It was something she held over me, whether on purpose I do not know. If I could not see it on one visit I nervously awaited the next and the next. Away from her I was a leader of men, with her, a boy.

There are more people out now but still I have not seen anyone I recognise and still I am not acknowledged. I cannot understand why this is. It is not possible for people to have forgotten.

I am a foreigner in my town. It is as if I am in my own home but after someone has come in and rearranged the furniture and upstairs in the bedroom is a woman asleep whom I have never seen before.

I do not have to walk very far to the kitchens. All the main buildings are very central. I wanted them arranged, as far as possible, close to the centre and close to the town hall. My own herding instinct I suppose. I round a corner and there it is. It hasn't changed at all. I can smell cooking even standing fifty metres away. I stand for a minute longer. Though I am hungry, I know that this is the time Tora used to work. I think what to say. I decide not to plan the exact words. I decide to let her say the first words. I walk up to the building but do not go inside. I walk around it, looking in the windows. Inside I can see benches and a few people sitting. There are women moving amongst them carrying platters of food and mugs of liquid. Very different to how it used to be done.

Some of the faces are familiar but again, there is no one whose name I know. And there is no sign of Tora. I do not know whether I am relieved or disappointed. Even if nothing else comes of this trip, for me to have seen her again is important. Yet, what will be behind the door if I open it? I have had years to forget her. I do not want to have to do it again. But I know I will seek her out. Indeed, if I am honest with myself, it is one of the main reasons I am back: to find the woman I love, to talk with her a while, to ask her questions, questions whose answers I have sought now for ten years. Perhaps to try to fix something broken, something that took up years of my life.

I push the door open and step inside with Andalus. I expect a silence to fall as I walk in but it does not. No one looks up from their meal. No one looks at all, except one of the serving women. Behind the counter at the far end I see her looking at me. I don't know what to do, whether the procedures are the same. I wonder whether I should confidently sit down and wait to be given food, whether I should explain at the outset why I might not be on the list of people to be given food, or whether I should simply wait here until someone comes to take me to a seat. In my day one formed a queue, had one's name ticked off in a register, sat down at one of the long wooden benches and was given food. But there is no food queue here. Suddenly the woman is in front of me.

'Hello,' she says. She smiles.

'Would you like to sit?' She points to an empty table. She looks at me but not at Andalus. It has been a while but the rituals come back to me now. The welcoming smile to a stranger, not an invitation but not a rebuttal either.

'Thank you,' I say. I sit down and she moves off. There are not many people in here. We are at a large table on our own. Two men are seated at the table on my left and are engaged in deep conversation. To my right are a woman and her child. She is feeding her. The child does not take her eyes off me.

I listen in on the conversation on my left. It is about nothing remarkable – weather and the harvest – on the surface at least. But these men seem to be expecting a plentiful crop and are arguing about the best way to trellis vines. This is the interesting aspect of it. The last time I was here there was only one way to trellis vines since we cared about quantity of fruit and nothing else. They argue about how growing methods affect the taste of the fruit.

I am pleased, proud in fact. The regulations I put into place, the strict laws, seem to have served their purpose. Rationing and farming controls and supervision, I am beginning to realise, are falling away, seemingly in response to improved production and increased quantity of food. My rules have rescued the settlement from starvation. It was a process you could see happening in my days as Marshal but I am surprised at how far it seems to have come, the fields of corn and wheat, the orange orchard and now this talk of abundant harvests of grapes.

Their conversation stops. They wait a few seconds before beginning another topic. I surmise they do not know each other very well.

I interrupt them. 'Excuse me,' I say. 'Your conversation about vines. I have been away for some time. When did you start caring about trellising?'

'What do you mean?' They answer me abruptly.

'Ten years ago we only grew vines one way.'

'We weren't here ten years ago. He has been here seven years, me five.'

Refugees, I think. I nod at them to thank them. But then I ask another question. 'Tell me about your Marshal. What's his name?'

They both turn to me with stern expressions. 'A good man,' one says. With that they both get up and move off.

The woman appears behind me, and leaning over my shoulder so I can smell her, whispers, 'Don't worry about them. They're not very talkative.' She places a bowl of soup in front of me and a beaker of red liquid. Not wanting to appear surprised I thank her and she goes away. I take a sip of the liquid and it is indeed wine. It is something that has never been freely available in my lifetime. Every now and then we would discover a cache of bottles, buried somewhere in ruins. Most was undrinkable. Occasionally some tasted fine. It was sweet. I probably drank one bottle a year and it was never handed out in the kitchens. A few of the bottles had labels. They had words

I didn't know, pictures I couldn't make out. Drinking the liquid was like drinking another world.

I realise Andalus has not been given food. I find it strange but am too distracted by the food in front of me to give it much thought. I do say to him though that he should ask for food if he wants some. He makes no sign of having heard.

The soup is hot and I finish it quickly. A plate then appears in front of me. It is piled high with meat and vegetables. I say nothing and just eat and drink. The wine brings a flush to my cheeks, the food warms me. I sit on the bench and I find myself smiling and I keep saying to myself you're home, you're home and I am grinning to myself while around me people eat, drink, talk and laugh.

When I finish I look around me to see what others do. I have not had my name taken. I notice other people getting up. They walk straight out the door, turning to wave goodbye at the servers. I too stand up. I walk past the woman on my way out. I stop opposite her. 'Thank you,' I say. I pause after the word 'you'.

She answers with a smile, 'Elba.'

I smile and nod. 'Thank you, Elba.'

Outside I sit on a bench with Andalus and lean forward, my head in my hands.

People walk around us, going about their business. I am still surprised there are not more people about but perhaps everyone is working in the fields. Children play in the street. No one gives the two old men on the bench in the town square a second glance.

This town square has a history. It is wide and surrounded on all sides by wooden buildings, one of which is the kitchen. We used the space to hold public gatherings. At the far end is a stage. I remember standing there one day. The square was packed. I believe every able-bodied citizen had come to listen. There were so many people that the dust kicked up by thousands of feet hung in the air above their heads. I was above the cloud of dust looking down on my people. I paused for breath and to take a sip of water. No one stirred. There was not a sound. That was when I knew I had them. I smiled inwardly. By way of conclusion I said, 'Once our kind was powerful, once we did not struggle. We will become strong again. It will not happen tomorrow, it will not happen next year but soon, soon we will become strong enough to ensure this will never happen again. There is no question of guilt here. No question at all. The most humane thing we can do is to ensure the survival of our children. The most humane thing we can do is to ensure the survival of a civilised way of life.'

There was no applause when I finished but I did not need it and it would have been inappropriate. My victory was inevitable. I had broken a barrier and I would now see out the plan for better or worse.

The audience would have known that many of them would end up hanged. Each would have known that either himself or the person standing next to him or behind him would end up dangling from a rope like a criminal. There was silence.

Many of them hung their heads. They did not look at each other. When they started leaving it seemed as if each person left separately. There were no groups, no families anymore. Everyone was on their own. They knew it was necessary. They knew what they had done.

Sometimes I wondered if my people wanted to hear about the past, whether they wanted to hear how all the evidence pointed to our kind being far more powerful, far more numerous and technologically advanced than we are now. Or whether they were only interested in what they had to do for an easier life, what they had to do to know where their next meal was coming from and how to survive in a harsh climate. I toned down my stories of ruins, of enormous boats and vessels, of papers covered in text no one could read, in favour of details of the food roster, the routine, the rules of the Programme. They were not interested in the poetry of the past, in how it can make us desire a new future. I though always knew that both were important – facts and stories. I used to think my people were overwhelmed by guilt and did not want to look beyond the here and now. I might have underestimated them.

Andalus has fallen asleep in the sun. Spittle runs from the side of his mouth.

I must find Tora. The apartment where she stayed is close by. Nothing, it is true, is very far from here. I wake Andalus and we walk around behind the kitchens and initially head in a southerly direction. Second right, first left, half-way down and there it is, a three-storey building, much like the others around it but special to me. I find another bench for Andalus and tell him to wait. He sits down without any fuss. I am surprised he is being so compliant in the home of his former enemy but I do not have time to think about that right now.

I walk up to the building and round the side. There I climb the stairs on the outside to the third floor. There are weeds growing in the cracks. It all looks exactly as I remember. I walk down the exterior passage passing six doors before I come to hers. Number thirty-seven. The number is still there, painted in the same way. The door is yellow.

The afternoon sun makes it seem as if it glows. I raise my hand and knock twice. My heart is beating hard. My mouth is dry. I feel like a child.

I hear nothing and knock again. This time though, I hear footsteps and a voice, a slightly breathless voice which says, 'Sorry, coming, I was washing …' and the door opens and the voice is not hers and I already know it is not Tora. But I am surprised to see the woman from the kitchen, Elba, standing before me, her hair still wet. She must have left straight after me. 'Oh, it's you,' she says. She does not seem as surprised as I am.

'Hello,' I say, 'I am sorry, I did not mean to disturb. I did not know you lived here. I was looking for someone.'

She looks expectantly at me but I hesitate. 'And?' she says, 'Have you found her?' I do not follow her meaning.

'She used to live here,' I say. 'She worked in the kitchens, like you. Do you know her?'

She tilts her head. 'I don't believe so. How long ago did she live here?'

'It was possibly as many as ten years, maybe fewer. I don't know.' I pause, 'I went away for a while.'

'That is strange,' she says. 'I have been here for eleven years and the flat was unoccupied before that. I'm not sure for how long.'

I realise she must have got her dates wrong. It is sometimes difficult to separate the years in this place. Sometimes it seems like a year has passed when in fact it is only a season. But I know I am not mistaken.

I ask her again. 'Her name is Tora. Did you know her perhaps?'

'I'm sorry.'

'Have you been working at the kitchens since you've lived here? If so your paths would have crossed.'

'Perhaps we did know each other and I have forgotten. People forget the strangest things.'

I smile at her. 'She is difficult to forget.'

She nods her head but makes no other reply.

'I have to ask,' I say. 'Do you know who I am?'

She looks at me with what I think is a smile on her face. 'I have never known you.'

It is a rather strange reply. I wonder briefly if she might be flirting. I try again, 'I don't look familiar to you?'

'I am sure I would not have forgotten you.'

I step back into the sunlight. I wonder how much I've changed. It seems I will have to seek Tora and Abel elsewhere. 'I am sorry to bother you,' I say.

She smiles and closes the door softly.

Andalus is where I have left him. I drag him to his feet.

It is now evening. Though I have not found Abel or Tora yet there is little more I can do tonight. I have nowhere to sleep and we need to find shelter. I am homeless in a town that should belong to me. We could head out into the orange groves but I do not want to find the gates closed again. I consider going back to the Marshal and asking for somewhere to stay. I also think of the woman living in Tora's flat but that would not be appropriate. I decide to walk around the town to see if I can find an abandoned house or some other form of shelter.

I walk in the direction of the administrative complex. After a few minutes I remember an alleyway that might serve our purposes. Before the complex I turn off to the right down a narrow passage. It turns to the left and continues for a few metres before widening into a little courtyard. There are no doors leading into it. With no through traffic this could be the best place to take shelter, at least until I have sorted things out here.

Against two of the walls are piles of furniture and boxes. There is a tarpaulin, which I drape over some of them.

I take the stone from my bag and hide it in a corner.

Andalus crawls into the shelter when I motion for him to do so. He lies down and pulls some papers over himself. As he crawls into the space between the canvas and wall I realise it is a very good hiding place. From a few steps back, as long as he makes no noise, you could never tell there is a huge man in the shadows. I tell him to be quiet, though by now I have given up expecting him to reply, and climb in after him.

I lie awake for a while listening to Andalus's faint breathing. A whole day has passed in my town. No one has recognised me. No one has even looked twice at me or at Andalus, though he sticks out. A big, pale mountain of a man amongst a people who are browner, earthier, closer to the ground. Even the Marshal, who should know better, did not react when he saw me. And, though I held back from saying who I was, he should have known. I am the one who brought stability to this town and it was only ten years ago that I was exiled. You would know me. Do people have such short memories? Do they choose not to see? It is vaguely unsettling, though it is better this way than to be hauled off to the gallows screaming my story, my excuse, to whomever will listen.

And Elba? There is something wrong with it. There are only a few thousand of us. You do not forget someone who lived in the flat before you, who had the same job, who is the same age. Or was.

Abel and Tora. One who sent me away. The other who brought me back. I will find them.

7

It is just before dawn when I wake. Andalus has thrown his arm around me. What do I feel for him, this man, this spectre? Truth is, I feel less and less. 'Feel' is not the right word. In the beginning I felt. I was frightened for a short time, then sympathetic, then angry. Until we left the island I veered between sympathy and compassion and loathing of his intrusion and his refusal to talk. The anger though was always tinged with guilt. Not only did I realise that perhaps what he had been through, whatever it was, had broken him but also I realised that he was my excuse, my passage off the island. His unwillingness to communicate, beyond the simplest of facial expressions, is useful in some respects. Perhaps if he had told the truth, blurted out his story, I would not have been able to justify leaving the island and bringing him to the attention of the settlement. His silence has been useful to me. I am not ignorant of my motives. But I must make him talk. And soon.

Lying in the semi-dark I wonder when I will first be recognised, acknowledged for what I am, for what I was. Who will be the first? Who will lift his eyes over his bowl of soup and stare at me? Will his jaw clench shut, his brow furrow? Will the room grow silent around me, me oblivious, lost in the hot food and the wine, and will I look up to see row upon row of men with black eyes staring at their ex-Marshal? Who will be the first to pick up a sickle and advance on me, shout at me, cut me down?

Or will it be a gentler thing, a flicker of recognition in the Marshal's eyes, a raised eyebrow and an 'Oh. It's you.'

Or will it be Tora who recognises me first? If I can find her then it will be her I am sure. She cannot have forgotten. No one forgets a man who shared your bed for near half a lifetime. No one forgets a man who provided for you. No one forgets a man who ordered your sole surviving relative to be hanged.

She forgave me for that.

She had to. It was written in statutes.

Besides, it was she who came to tell me of her mother's incapacity, she who stood aside for the hangman.

I forgave her for that.

I had to. It was me who forced her to abandon her mother, forced her to betray one she loved.

I did not think much about why she had done it. It was what everyone did. But Tora was different. She was the one who had said 'Rather die than be tainted by the murder of your own people.' I should have asked her why. I should have thought more about why she did it, more about what was behind the unblinking eyes. So many things I should have done. I can only guess now.

I think back to when I held her that night, the first time she came to me after her mother's death. Did she whisper something? Did she say to me, 'She had suffered enough. She would have wanted release'?

I think. I hear something. It might be only the wind outside blowing dust through the streets.

It took her four days to come and tell me. Longer than she should have delayed. What was she going through in that time?

I cannot believe Tora would have been like the others. Not she. Cold. Weak. I want to believe. I cannot not believe she would have had another reason, some explanation. I could not have turned her so. Stripped her.

I throw off Andalus's arm and crawl out of the shelter. He follows, yawning. I tell him to stay in the shelter. He does not move but also does not follow me when I leave the alleyway. I will take him with me later but for now I am better off on my own. I can move more quickly without him.

I will go to Abel's house. If anyone can rectify the current situation it is he. I am curious to find out why he is not still the Marshal. Though it is an elected post, we did not have set periods for elections. Death or, it seems, banishment, were our reasons for new elections. When a people is faced with an issue serious enough to threaten their livelihood, they do not bother with nuanced political visions, they do not bother with who is more right, who is morally better. They require only a strong leader, a leader with a clear vision and awareness. They also do not need to waste their energy arguing with each other over trifles such as election periods. Our people are not used to change and Abel was perfect to come after me, to live on the legacy I created for many years. Strong, forthright and a traditionalist, he should have been exactly what this town needed.

But people change. I have already seen evidence of this. Perhaps with the easing of the burdens they had to carry, they have more time to ponder, more time to be dissatisfied, more time to change their minds. I am sure though Abel would not have gone without a fight.

I remember his house very clearly, its walls made from the same bleached-grey wood as the rest of the buildings, strengthened here and there with mud baked solid. I often strolled past it on my daily walks around the town. These would take me from the town hall to the main gate and then in an anti-clockwise direction. It took me an hour and a half for the five miles. Smaller than my island. His house was three-quarters of the way round, set back from the walls, the entrance down a narrow passage. I would sometimes glance down it when I walked, at the one window visible from the street.

Every now and then I saw Abel through the window or coming out or going in. I would wave. I would very rarely stop. We spent the whole day together and did not need to talk more than that. Towards the end I saw other officials there too on one occasion. It was late. I was in the shadow of the wall and I do not think I was seen. When his guests were gone he was framed in light from the doorway. I moved and my feet crunched against the gravel. 'Who's there?' he called out. I did not answer. Though he was looking in my direction I know he did not see me. If he had, he would have greeted me. I knew all of them – I had appointed them after all – so why didn't I make myself known? Though I did not allow the thought to surface then, I knew. Suspicion begins in the marrow. That night was the start of it all, months before anything happened, months before I was arrested.

I think I wanted to scare him a little, though I didn't yet realise why of course. I wanted him to be afraid of the shadows, of what might be out there. But it is only people with imagination who can be afraid and I have always felt he was lacking in that area. It is I who imagined a better life. He executed orders. I wouldn't call his plot imaginative. Expedient yes, imaginative no.

As I walk around the town walls, I glance over my shoulder to see if anyone is looking and trail my fingers across the wooden walls. I would do this sometimes. I like the touch, the tangible sense that what these walls contained was dependent on me. I also liked that every time I ran my fingers over the wall, fragments, splinters would fall to the ground. Every time a little of the wall was destroyed. That is the instinct of one who is afraid of heights: you do not want to but you feel drawn to the edge, feel an urge to jump.

I never saw Tora leaving that house.

Almost before I know I am upon it, I am standing at the entrance to the alleyway. I look through the window but a shade covers it and I can see nothing. I move down the alley and knock on the door, loudly, three times. There is no answer. The door rattles on its hinges. It would not take much to kick it in.

I lean down to try to see through the opening at the bottom of the door. I look through the keyhole but it is blocked and I can see only a faint glimmer of light. A key on the inside maybe. I stand and wait. I wait for five minutes or more. I press my ear to the door and knock lightly this time.

I become aware of a man standing at the head of the alleyway. He is old. He has his arms at his sides. He looks at me. He does not blink and his mouth is open. I stand up straight. I take a step towards him. My mouth too is open. I take another step and he has turned on his heel and is running. From the entrance to the alley I watch him. He runs like an old man. I take a deep breath, smile and run after him. I tell myself not to hurt him when I catch him.

He is old but not as slow as I thought he would be. Every time I think I'm catching him he disappears round another corner. He weaves in and out of buildings. I do not shout out to him. He knows I know him.

I struggle to contain the anger rising in me.

I fly around a corner and run straight into a man. I am knocked flat. He has held out a stiffened arm. He does not say anything, this man. I cannot see. I am dazed but I sense he just looks at me lying on the ground. Then he walks off. I get up slowly, first to my knees then to my feet. I call to him, 'You!' I shout. He pretends not to hear. I lean against the wall and recover my breath.

I have lost the other, the old man, the judge, the one who, acting on orders from Abel, banished me from the settlement of Bran.

I walk back to Abel's house. I am surprised at my feelings when I saw the judge. He is not someone I have blamed before for sending me away and I don't know what I would have done if I had caught him.

But I am pleased nonetheless. I have seen someone from the past, someone whose name I know and not just dimly recognise. He is here. And I am certain he recognised me. For now, that is enough.

Limping slightly I move off to sit in the shade of the wall near Abel's house. There is a bench and I sit and wait for him to come home, or to leave it.

But nothing happens. Nothing at all. The street is quiet. When people pass sometimes they look at me only to look away quickly. It is fleeting but I do not imagine this. Sometimes they do not seem to notice me at all. A few children run after each other. Mostly there are no people in the street at all. More significantly, there is no movement in the house, or none that I can notice. The curtain does not twitch, the door does not open. I sit in the shade with my head resting against the wall. A fly settles on my forehead and I brush it away. I feel the sun on my face, on my skin, and my eyes close.

Abel. It is a common name in Bran. Its origins are unclear but we tell of two brothers at the beginning of time. Abel is murdered by his brother. He is the victim of the first evil. Why we would name our children after victims I have never understood. The tale tells of a man who takes his brother into a field. The man is jealous of his younger brother. Of what precisely he does not know. Of the fact that he is younger. He waits till his back is turned, picks up a stone. As he does the act, striking blow after blow, crows rise as one from the field, startled. Hundreds of them. They don't make a sound. Or if they do he cannot hear. They blacken the skies above. The red earth stretches from horizon to horizon.

Abel was not a victim.

The judge sits on a raised platform. Behind him is the wall on which, beneath the heading 'Marshals of Bran', is inscribed my name and the date 'Bran, BI'. He begins to speak, 'Marshal Bran, you are hereby sentenced to exile in perpetuity. You will be given a boat, provisions. You are to set sail, due east. If you find land before the territory of Axum, then that is where you should stay. If you do not, then you must take your chances in Axum. Under no circumstances are you to return to Bran. If you do you will be executed. The people's court has decided to spare you the fate that you dealt out with the utmost willingness. You have shown no remorse for your actions even though it is clear you are alone in pursuing the policies. You will never be forgiven by this town for we hereby expunge you.' He folds his hands in front of him, leans slightly forward. 'You were once a warrior, once a man with vision. Now ...' He pauses, and leans back. 'Now, do not come back.' With that he waves his hands and soldiers come and take me by the arms, quite gently, and lead me back to the cell. The court is silent. I turn to look over my shoulder. Abel is standing in the gallery. He is shaking the hands of the men next to him. He will not meet my eye. Tora is not there. The next time I see her is my last day in the town for ten years.

I am woken by a hand on my shoulder. I look up, still half asleep. The sun is behind her face. A yellow glow comes from her hair. At first I think it is my lover. I sit up straight. It is not. It is Elba.

'Good morning,' she says. I have not slept for long.

'Yes. Hello.' I am still a bit confused.

'You're enjoying the sun?'

'I am tired. I have had a long journey. Maybe it is catching up with me now.'

She moves out of the sun and sits next to me. Her skin is flushed. 'Are you hungry?'

'I am.'

'Come to the kitchens with me then.'

We get up from the bench and start to walk slowly towards the kitchens. I ask, 'Have you remembered Tora yet?'

'Have I remembered who?' She answers this very quickly.

'Have you remembered the person of whom I spoke?'

She smiles at me. I find this a little frustrating but her smile makes her seem younger than she is. It brightens her. 'I am sorry.'

I stare at her for a few seconds. 'You know who I am.' It is not a question.

'I am sorry. You have not told me your name.'

I ignore this. 'I saw the judge this morning.' I look closely at her. She does not answer. 'The judge. From ten years ago.'

She looks ahead. 'What would you like to eat?' is all she says but she takes me by the arm. I am silent.

In the kitchens she says, 'Sit anywhere you like.'

I watch her as she walks away. She is not old but not in the prime of her life either. I wonder if she has a husband, a lover. I turn back, remembering Tora.

When she returns with food and has placed it in front of me, instead of leaving she remains standing. I pause in the act of lifting my fork to my mouth. 'Do you mind?' she says, pointing to the seat next to me.

'Not at all,' I say and make as if to pull the chair out for her but she gets there first and in my haste I knock my knife to the floor.

'Thank you,' she says and takes a clean knife from one of the other settings and places it in front of me. It is an unfussy movement, making light of my clumsiness. She would make a good wife.

For a few seconds I do not know what to do.

'Not hungry?' She asks, pointing to the food.

'Oh, yes,' I say, and smile.

'Was she an old lover of yours?' I am slightly taken aback by the forwardness of the question but not for long. I decide to answer truthfully.

'Yes. She was my lover for twelve years before I went away. Twelve happy years.'

A serious expression comes over her face. 'Why did you go away?'

If there is a game with this woman she is good at playing it. For a moment I wonder whether I have changed more than I think. Perhaps ten years in the rain have altered me. I am certainly slimmer and probably a lot darker. It is as if the peat has soaked into me, through my feet, staining my skin a dark brown.

'I was sent away.' I watch for a change in expression but there is none.

'Why?'

'The courts sent me away. The judge.'

'Ah, you're one of our ambassadors. You have been away a long time? It seems as if you have.'

'Why is that?' I do not show my surprise at her talking of ambassadors.

'You seem …' She pauses. 'Perhaps things have changed a bit in the last few years. You will get used to us soon again.'

'Yes,' I say. 'Yes, I probably will.' I stare into her eyes, slightly longer than is necessary.

'How long were you away?'

'Ten years.' I am still staring at her. She drops her eyes from my gaze and hesitates.

'And the woman? Why didn't she go with you?'

'It would not have been right.'

'Forgive me,' she says. 'I ask too many questions.' She begins to get up as if to leave. Without thinking I grab her wrist.

'Stay. Please. I mean, if you don't have any work to do.' She sits again. 'I told you she used to work here.'

'Yes, I remember you saying but I do not remember someone called Tora. I have been here almost twelve years. No Tora.'

'She started these kitchens. She was the first one to organise the meal rota.'

She shrugs, 'Sorry.'

'She looked a bit like you,' I say. She looks away again.

'What will you do if you find her?'

'If I find her?' Now I pause. 'It has been a long time. I don't know. It depends on the first meeting, I think. Then I will know what to do.' I do not tell her that Tora was the only person I have ever loved. I do not tell her of the trial, though I am convinced she knows about that. How could she not? I do not tell her of Abel. I do not tell her of the island. Soon though. I will tell her why I came back. I feel this with some certainty.

But I truly don't know what I will do when I see Tora.

The woman senses my change in mood. 'I should get back to work,' she says.

I want to keep her as an ally. 'Forgive me,' I say. 'I do not mean to be rude. I would like to talk again. Would you mind if I called on you?'

She looks around, as if shy. 'I don't work nights. You could come this evening.' She turns to walk away but stops, then turns back.

She stoops to talk to me and whispers, 'You shouldn't go chasing men through the streets. We don't like that sort of thing. It will not be good for you.' She walks off before I have a chance to respond.

I make my way to the Marshal's office. On the way I go to the shelter to find Andalus. I give him some food I took from the kitchens.

When he is done I lead him to the courtyard of the administrative complex. Again there is no one around. I walk up to the Marshal's door and knock. There is still no reply to the second knock. It is the middle of the day and the office should be open now. Even if the Marshal is not in, there should be clerks and officials about. A settlement cannot function without its administration. The townspeople though do not seem to care. It is a somnolent place, much changed since I left. There are few people on the streets. How many people have died, I wonder. With the area so fertile I doubt it is possible for a town's citizenry to be entirely replaced by a new one. Almost no one around and many of those I do see appear furtive, they shuffle around barely glancing up and when they do they hurriedly look away. Apart from the children, proof that the town is not dying. And the woman from the kitchens. There's a story in her, that I can sense. But there is a distance about her. She is far away.

I open my palm and bang on the door. I can hear an echo. I try the handle but it is locked. I turn to go and Andalus is right behind me. I have to pull up to avoid bumping into him. 'Do you want to try?' I push him towards the door. He stands in front of it doing nothing. Then he turns his head slowly towards me. Is he shaking his head? I cannot see. He is standing in the shadows, I in the sun. I cannot see him.

I leave him to follow me. We go back to the shelter and I lie down. I will try again later. I will not criticise. I will remain civil. My case will be difficult enough to state without my losing my temper.

Speech from Andalus would make it so much easier. 'People of Bran,' I imagine him saying, 'My land, Axum, is under siege from a band of people neither of us has come across before. I escaped because I was out on a surveying trip when they attacked. I tried to go back to rescue Axum but I could not get past. I thought of Bran, once an enemy, now an ally. On the way to find help I got lost at sea. These people, the third band, could well be on their way here right now. For all we know they could be sweeping over the hills in the night, eyes glowing red from the dust kicked up by the heels of thousands. They are strong. They will not rest until Bran and Axum are slaughtered. They are the new breed. We can defeat them but only if we unite.' How easy would it be then for me to get what I came for.

A third force. More people. Perhaps a blessing. Probably a curse. The world is so vast, our memory of it so small. Everything we see, all new lands we come across, each new set of ruins; new, yet we always feel like we've seen them before, like we've been there before. We are a group of people who have lost their memory but retain a sense of having been. Once we were kings. Now it appears a terrible accident, an extinction, a curse has wiped our memories clean. Almost clean. Every now and then something from below pokes its head above the surface, like the people I imagine crawling up from underground into the smoke. It sickens you to think of what might have been.

Could others be closer than we think? We have explored much but there was always more to see. Maybe we missed them. I think this often. Untouched by our curse, a village with green grass, smoke coming from chimneys, fat children singing.

My people seemed afraid of the search, of the ruins, of finding something new. I had evidence for that but chose not to see it. My stories fell on deaf ears. Few wanted to hear about the ruins, about pictures that I found, strange artefacts half buried in the dust. Once we were marching through an area of desert. We walked towards what we thought was a tree in the distance. It was a stone pillar. At the base was an entrance leading underground. My men hung back. I asked for volunteers to go with me. Each man hung his head. 'I will go alone then. I will show you there is nothing to fear.' I took a torch. One man begged me to stay. In fact he grabbed my arm. I pushed him away and ordered them to make camp.

I descended stone stairs. The torch flickered on the walls. It was cool below ground in spite of the heat of the torch. The passage went further underground and turned corners. I marked my way with a stone. I had been walking for a long time when I began to see them. Shelves set into the walls. On each shelf a body, some wrapped in cloths, some not. I walked deeper into the cavern. Hundreds and hundreds of them stretching from my feet to above my head on both sides of the walls.

I came at last to a circular chamber. There on a stone slab a piece of metal in the shape of a cross. There was a red stone in the middle of it. It flickered in the fire.

It was cold in there and I left, hurrying out. I did not know what to make of it and I left it feeling dumb. Too many stories to be told, even for me.

Outside the men would not meet my eyes. They were silent. I did not tell them what I had seen. It was three days before they recovered their humour.

Later in the afternoon I go back to the Marshal's office, this time on my own. I spend a long time waiting, knocking, shouting. I kick the door once. The sun sets and I leave. I will not let the Marshal avoid me. I will have my say.

I make my way to Elba's flat alone. In the settlement lights come on in windows, flickering behind curtains, barely lighting the street. Shapes move past the lights, past yellow drawn curtains, hover like spirits before fading into black. I sense more of them, figures moving behind the walls, trying not to make a sound.

Not dead then.

I walk the long way to her flat and see few people out. I come to a place in the wall where you can climb up to the ramparts. It is normally guarded but now there is no one here. The gate is on a latch, not locked. I lift it and walk through, climbing the narrow stairs. I used to come here sometimes, at night mostly, still summer nights. Looking out over the town, the quiet darkened town, I can see all of it. I can see the town hall. I can see the walls and the grey wooden buildings that have stood for so long, the architecture of a people with little imagination, little will to better themselves. I was torn, I remember, between fatherly feelings, between wanting to protect this mongrel people and anger at the lack of imagination, at the lack of will to do something out of the ordinary, to be extraordinary. A failure of imagination. I felt anger, sometimes, that it was left to me, a stronger mind, to lead, to imagine, to impose something like order on these simple people. I wondered if it was worth it. To have saved a savage is perhaps no great thing after all.

It is true, they did imagine something different for a while. But were they true believers or simply believing for the sake of expediency? I fear the latter. But then sometimes, at night, lying awake, I too sometimes stopped believing. I never told anyone that. Too late though. I stopped believing too late. Too late to stop the faces coming to me in the dark, to stop the screaming of the children in the island night.

I have achieved little since coming back. I have not told my story,

I have not found Tora or Abel. I need a reaction in order to know what to do. Somewhere in the town, somewhere in a building I can see will lie the answer, will lie my future. Somewhere in the town if alive, or somewhere just beyond the walls if dead, lie their bodies, my touchstones. Breathing or decaying, breath or fetid airs, their fumes I imagine wafting in the warm breeze, drifting here to my nostrils. I could follow them like a dog follows its prey. So close.

But not close enough. I have come home after a long absence and my children have made rules of their own. The patriarch has returned but his children no longer know who he is. Or admit to know.

If I don't get a reaction soon I will have to take matters into my own hands.

8

I am surprised when the door opens. It is opened not by Elba but by a girl. She has large brown eyes. I am struck by them. They remind me of mine when I was a boy. It is the same girl I saw when entering the town for the first time.

'Hello,' I say. 'What is your name?' I lean down to her.

She turns her face away from me and walks into the flat leaving the door open. Elba appears. 'This is my daughter,' she says. 'Tell the man your name.'

The girl looks up and says boldly, almost haughtily, 'My name is Amhara.'

I did not expect Elba to have a child. She had not mentioned it before. But then why would she? In the settlement children spend a long time away from their parents. They are schooled intensively and live in boarding houses for most of the week. That way we could both accelerate their learning and ensure that each was provided for equally and adequately. I presume that at least has not altered since my time.

'That is a beautiful name.' I say in response. 'And how old are you?'

'Nine.'

I will admit disappointment at the fact that Elba has a daughter. Though I do not expect much of her, it will mean that her loyalties will never be totally with me.

'I did not mention her to you as it did not come up,' Elba says, as if reading my thoughts.

'Oh,' I say, 'nothing to be concerned about.' I don't know what to say. 'You have a very beautiful daughter.'

Luckily Elba smiles at that point and asks if I would like to come inside.

For a while we talk while the child draws on a sheet of paper at the table. The conversation is slightly awkward. She asks after a pause, 'You seem to be wondering about her,' nodding towards the girl. It is more of a statement than a question. In fact I have not wondered much at all. It would be unusual to see a woman of a certain age without a child in our settlement and there do seem to be a lot of them around now. Tora did not have one. She was different in that way. I suppose you could say she was allowed certain favours, being the lover of the Marshal.

'Where's the father?' I ask.

She pauses and does not look me in the eye. 'He left,' she says simply. 'He went away. He is still alive but he won't come back. Not truly.'

I want to ask what she means but she carries on.

'He would not be a good father anyway. Too flighty, too angry. I do not mean physically, not that kind of anger. An anger against the world. Though he had things just so, though he was very successful in our way, he was angry. To say he went voluntarily would not be true. He could not have stayed. Others began to sense it. It was like he was always looking for something else, somewhere else. This place was not for him.'

'Where is he?'

She does not answer. Her head is bent over.

'He named her.' She says suddenly, pointing at Amhara. 'At least, he suggested the name. He left before she was born. A long-dead people who once ruled the world only for time to turn their monuments into ruins. That's what he said anyway, I have never heard of them. There was much knowledge of the past he claimed to have.' She was beginning to sound bitter.

'Still,' she says more calmly, 'without the history, it is a beautiful name. It is like the wind at night.'

I smile at her quaint expression. The Amhara people are indeed another of our rumours. I remember telling Tora about some evidence I discovered: a stone monolith engraved with a phrase. There were two scripts. The one I could decipher read, 'We, the Amhara …' The rock was chipped at that point and the rest of the sentence lost. I scratched around in the dust but could find no more.

'You laugh,' she says, smiling herself. Her gaze meets mine for a moment, then we both look at the child.

She changes the subject, 'You say you too have been away. Where, with whom, doing what?'

I take a deep breath. I decide to play along for now. 'I left ten years ago,' I begin. 'Ten years ago I lived in this town. I was an important man. It seems people have forgotten me. Our people have always had a lot to think about so I do not begrudge them their forgetfulness.' I want to make sure she knows I do not blame her for the town's collective memory loss.

I continue while we eat. 'I left … The truth is I was asked to leave. The settlement had changed. They thought I was no longer able to lead them into the next phase of the recovery. They thought there was a need for a change. Or they were made to think that way by treacherous people close to me. They thought the policies that had served us so well for the previous ten years were no longer warranted. Or so they said. The fact of the matter is they could not admit that I had saved the settlement with these policies and given them all a sense of meaning and that they had been right behind the policies when it suited them. They could not admit their culpability for the deaths that took place beyond the city walls where the orange groves now stand. An interesting point that, I think. Where people previously lost their lives for the greater good now stands a fertile grove of fruit trees. Is that remembering the dead properly? Maybe it is.'

I realise I have gone off topic and Elba is looking at me strangely with her head cocked to one side.

I continue: 'I went to an island just inside the settlement limits on the border we agreed with Andalus of Axum. And there I stayed for a decade. I found I could live off the island well enough. Though it rained nearly every day and I do not believe I saw the sun once, it was not too bad. It was never very cold and I found enough peat and enough food to keep myself going. I did not cultivate anything as there was no point, it being just me. I also realised that the island was winding down. Like an old man it had a number of years left to live but no more. In the north the cliffs were falling rapidly into the sea. Virtually every day a section would collapse. The water round that end was always black with the mud. I would fancy that it was like blood, that the cliffs were men falling one by one to be broken by the sea.

'After a while I realised that the trees were infertile and weren't replenishing themselves. I realised the fish were becoming more scarce, that the peat bogs were not as extensive as they seemed. I calculated – and I made many calculations – instead of planting. I made notes and wrote down observations and sums. I worked out that the island had about as many years left to live as I did. My death would coincide with the end of the island as a viable source of support. And I preferred it that way. I was, I thought, resigned to the island being my resting place. I was resigned to never seeing this place again. There was a pace of life that appealed. The routines, the endless rains, the wet grasses brushing against my skin, the silence of the forest. Though I was alone it was a better life than you might think.'

'Why then did you leave the island?' Elba asks.

'Why did I leave?' I repeat her question almost to myself. 'I left because something happened that changed all that. One day I came across a man who had washed up on the shore. He was lying on the beach, almost dead. I gave him back life, took care of him but he had been through a trauma of some kind and would not speak. He did not say a word. As silent as a stone. To this day he has not said anything and it has been several weeks since he first appeared on my island.

'But this was no ordinary man. Though I did not recognise who it was at first, after a while I realised that this was no less than Andalus, General of Axum, with whom I had negotiated our peace. I then realised the significance of why he might be there, of the immense danger our people might face. There were always those factions within the Axumites who disapproved of the Peace Treaty. If they got the upper hand and ousted Andalus, there would be no doubt where they would turn their attentions next and I feared our people had become weak after years without war. Or, though it seems fanciful, what if there were other people entirely who ousted him? Even if he wasn't overthrown, what was he, a General, doing out there? Exploring? Looking for new territories? Something which is strictly against the terms of the treaty. Something had to be done. Our people had to be warned.'

Out of the corner of my eye I notice the child looking at me, staring at me in fact. Elba notices too and says quickly, 'Bedtime.' She takes Amhara by the hand and leads her through to the back of the apartment without a word to me.

When she returns, she says simply, 'She seems to like your stories.'

I do not say anything.

Then she says, shaking her head quickly as if remembering something, 'You've come into my home, told me a story, met my daughter and yet I don't even know what you want me to call you.'

I can't help but scoff. I hold my hand up to apologise. She sits down again and I lean in to her. 'You have been very kind to me but I must ask, I must know.' I pause. 'You surely know who I am?'

She shakes her head. 'Who are you?'

'I am Bran of course.'

She smiles again. 'Like our town, I like that.'

I lean back again and sigh. 'Elba, I would like you to help me understand what is going on. I would like you to tell me why it is that no one here has acknowledged me, why no one has admitted to recognising me? I was the ruler of this settlement for a long time, a man many grew to despise, and yet nothing. And where is everyone? Everyone I knew. Is this a town of ghosts?' I realise my voice is slightly raised. Again I hold up my hand.

Elba looks at me from across the table, then gets up and stands with her back to me, her arms folded.

After a few moments, when it seems like she is not going to answer,

I ask, 'How did you know what happened this morning? I did not tell you.'

'People talk.' She shrugs her shoulders. Then, 'I heard it mentioned that someone was chasing someone else through the streets. I assumed it was you.'

This is not a reasonable explanation but I cannot push her too hard, not yet. She is my best potential source of information so far.

'The man I was chasing was the judge at my trial. He is the first person I've been able to put a name to. Some people here seem vaguely familiar, like the Marshal, who I think was someone I used to know. Though some are familiar, it is like everyone I knew well has disappeared.'

She says nothing.

'And what of the person who lived in this flat before you? I cannot believe you wouldn't know her. And Abel, the man who became Marshal after me, the one who led the campaign against me? You must know them. Where are they?'

'The memory plays tricks sometimes. It can tell you you're one thing when actually you're another. Sometimes you discover you have an entirely different past to what you believed.'

'Is there something going on I should know about? Is there a plan being cooked up for how to deal with me? I realise I have probably brought confusion to your midst. I am not asking to come back as Marshal. I am not even asking to come back. I am asking for … There are things I've done …' I stumble.

'What are you asking for? What have you done, Bran?'

'I need to be able to speak to the Marshal about this. But he was not at his post yesterday even though we had an appointment. It's irregular. The world is broken, Elba. You will not survive without strong leadership and a man who abandons his duties is not a strong leader.'

'The strong sometimes know very little about strength.'

I do not know what she means. She turns around quickly and says, 'It is late. I have an early start. I think you should go now.'

I am being dismissed, perhaps a bit curtly too. At the door though, she takes me by the arm. She speaks softly, 'Though I cannot help you, you will have your answers one day. I'm certain of it.' With this she closes the door and I am left in the cool night.

I wander slowly back towards the shelter. The town is dark. There is no moon. Around me a few shapes flit through the dark, their heads buried in cloaks. I grab one by the shoulder as he shuffles past. I spin him around and the hood falls from his head. A blank face. 'Do you know me?' I ask. I speak from the back of my throat. He shakes his head. 'Do you know Bran?' He shakes his head, tries to pull away. 'Ten years ago –'

He interrupts me. 'I was not here.' He wrenches himself free and slides back into the dark.

When I am within sight of the town hall I see a figure hurry into the courtyard. I don't think he sees me. I recognise the gait and stature of the Marshal and I hurry after him. When I reach the courtyard there is no one in it. A glow from a lamp in the centre illuminates, dimly, the surrounding buildings.

I walk up to the Marshal's door and am about to knock but I lower my hand and try the door instead. It is open.

My eyes have to adjust to the gloom inside. Once they do I see that the floor is coated in a thin layer of dust. It is on everything. The dust gets everywhere in this town. I look down at the floor and try to make out the Marshal's prints. But there is nothing. He must have gone through another door. Most of the offices connect so I could still find him. I will be quiet though. I might be able to find evidence of what's going on if no one knows I'm here.

If I walk through the building now they will know from the footprints that someone has been in. But that is alright. They should know. I head up the stairs. They creak, but so lightly someone standing a few paces off would not be able to hear. I pass the landing with a window overlooking the courtyard. I freeze. There is a man standing below looking at the door. He would not be able to see me. I cannot make him out, cannot see his face. He stands there for what seems like minutes, not moving, just staring at the door. Suddenly he turns and walks out of the courtyard. I wait for a while but he does not return.

I walk up to my old office. The door is closed and locked. I carry on down the passageway. The next room is one I used for my assistants. This too is locked. The third room was used in my day by Abel. The current Marshal does not seem to have a deputy. This door is wide open. Inside everything is covered by sheets. I pull one off the desk. It is the same. I know because I had it made. It was a present to Abel when I made him deputy. I try one of the drawers. Locked. I pull at it but the handle breaks off.

I must face the possibility that both he and Tora are dead. That would be unlucky certainly, for both of the people I know best to die within my period of absence. Perhaps they were together when they died. They would have been together quite often I suppose after I left, sharing what they did. But with no wars anymore, little crime, enough food so it seems, why would they die? They were both young. Younger than I am anyway. They cannot both have died.

There on the side of the desk, the motto of Bran: In unity, strength. The wood is worn from use.

I pull off the sheet from the bookshelf. There, a copy of the constitution of the settlement. Abel and I wrote this together.

I walk out of the room after replacing the sheets. Further down the corridor are more offices. Because we built in a random fashion and added bits to buildings when we needed to without regard for a grand design, the corridor is not straight. It turns, doubles back on itself. With no windows it is dark inside. You could lose yourself in here if you didn't know what you were doing. I walk through the building trying all the doors. Abel's office is the only one unlocked. I regret leaving my knife in the shelter. I usually have it. With it I could have forced a lock. I could push in the doors but that would make a lot of noise.

I return the way I came and instead of going through the front door, turn left. I push open the doors to the hall. There is something I want to see. The room is empty. This is not unusual, it often was. Only for big meetings would we spread out the chairs. I walk towards the far end. There is a stage and to the left a wall panelled with wood. My footsteps, though cushioned by the dust, echo round the room. Gold lettering appears out of the gloom as I get close. At the top it reads, simply, 'Marshals of Bran'. Below are just two names. I peer closely at them. It is like my heart stops. My name is not there. The first entry should be 'Bran' followed by the years I ruled but instead the first entry is Madara. The years are the same, B1 to B10. The second name is Abel. That is right but then what of Marshal Jura? Why no inscription for the current Marshal? And if the decision was taken to expunge the name of a Marshal convicted of wrongdoing, why replace my name with a fictional one? No matter what they thought of me, they cannot forget my achievements. And besides, they all know they are guilty too. Yes I was banished but out of guilt, not hatred. There were some who hated of course but it was mostly guilt. I feel a rage inside me, something I have not felt for years, not since the battlefield and even then infrequently. In a battle the angry lose, the detached win. I calm myself as I walk through the door and out into the cold air, though I notice I have been sweating. I wipe my forehead with the back of my hand.

I decide against exploring further tonight. Tomorrow I will make sure I have an audience with the Marshal.

Madara. A name. A fictional name. A word whose presence means that the settlement has an imperfect history. Why not keep the true name? Even if you hate the name and what it stands for, at least recognise it, stare it in the face.

Madara. It is familiar somehow. A name I once heard. A person I once knew. I am not Madara.

I walk around the town for hours. I walk past Elba's windows. There is a light on in one. I watch it for a few minutes. A shadow moves across the yellow blinds, floats across the space, back and forth, back and forth as if in a dance.

I walk past Abel's house. That, in contrast, is still dark. It is very late, however. It means little.

I walk past the courtyard entrance. Twice, three times.

The third time I look up at the windows. Behind one there is a movement. I am almost certain there is someone, a pale figure deep in the shadows, staring out, looking at me. I stare harder but there is nothing more. I go further into the courtyard, look up. The window is black.

I think back to the figure I saw in the courtyard earlier. He too was looking up at the windows. Was he waiting for a signal from a figure behind one? Was he looking for me?

As I notice a lightening in the sky, I walk back to the shelter. Andalus is snoring slightly, his hands spread across his belly as if he has been feasting splendidly. I sit outside, my back to the wall, close my eyes and wait for the sun to creep up the alleyway.

9

I sleep for a short time. I wake when people should be starting the working day. Andalus has not eaten the food I brought back. I help myself to half of it.

He is awake. I say to him, 'We are going to the Marshal's office now. I will get answers from him. It will be easier if you talk.' He sits with his hands on his legs, palms upwards. His feet are within touching distance. Sun glints through tears in the canvas behind him.

'You need to explain yourself, my friend. I cannot look after you forever. Sooner or later you will be on your own.'

It is no surprise to me when he does not answer.

We go out into the sunshine and walk the short distance to the complex. There are four people in the courtyard of the town hall. The Marshal is in conversation with another man. He is tall, wears a hood and I cannot see any of his features. The Marshal is the only one who faces me. The other two, I am convinced, are Elba and Amhara. Though it is a little distance away and they have their backs to me and are wearing scarves over their heads, I am convinced. As soon as I enter the courtyard the Marshal notices me. He seems to whisper something to the three. They straighten up but do not turn. They walk through the open door behind the Marshal, the tall man leading the other two. The girl seems to hang back and begins to turn but the woman places a hand on her back and guides her through the door, which closes after them.

The Marshal waits for me, his hands crossed in front of him, unlike a soldier.

'What can I help you with today?' he asks.

Enough is enough, I decide. 'We had an appointment yesterday.'

'Did we?'

'You mean to say you don't remember?'

He shrugs.

'Do you recognise me yet?' I ask. I wonder if he notes my sarcastic tone. 'You have had time to think, time to remember. I do not, I'm afraid, recognise you. You were perhaps a minor official when I left.'

The Marshal remains standing, not answering my question, waiting for me to finish.

'I think you know who I am,' I continue. 'I think you know very well. What I can't decide is why you would choose not to acknowledge me. Throughout my life I have been either hero or villain, depending on your political leanings. I have never been an object of indifference.'

The Marshal allows a smile to cross his lips.

'But I am not the only issue here. The man I brought with me is one that has to be reckoned with. He is perhaps now of little use, of little consequence. Perhaps what he has seen has driven the life force from him but what he represents is important. The possibilities encased in his being here are what should be of interest. Perhaps the man Andalus is gone but we should understand why there is that void, the void in the space where he stands.'

144

'You're a philosopher,' says the Marshal. 'Or a poet.'

I do not respond to this.

'Where is this man, then, this Andalus?' He emphasises the second syllable, whereas he should know to emphasise the third. It is a mistake some of my less well-informed people used to make.

I do not correct him. I turn around, reaching out to Andalus who I assume is behind me. He is not. There is no sign of him.

I turn back to the Marshal. 'He was here. He has wandered off.'

The Marshal smiles and turns to go.

'I am not finished,' I say. I have raised my voice.

He turns back. The smile has vanished.

'Where are Elba and Amhara?'

'Who do you mean?'

'You know she doesn't want to be a part of your plan. Hesitant at the very least.'

The Marshal looks at me without replying. His face is blank.

'I saw them go inside.'

'They are not who you say they are.'

I decide not to pursue that. Instead I say, 'I would like to talk about my situation. I would like a decision from you. A deadline, at the least.'

'You would like to talk,' says the Marshal. It is not a question.

Before I can reply he stands aside and motions me through the door.

I walk straight ahead towards the staircase leading to the Marshal's office. There is no sign of Elba and Amhara. Through a corridor I see the hall I was in last night. I think about going straight in there and questioning the meaning of the erasure of my name. But that can wait.

I walk up the stairs, past the doors to offices belonging to clerks and lower officials and straight through the door to the Marshal's office. Inside, things have changed slightly. There is a rug on the floor that wasn't there before and a cabinet against the right-hand wall. I notice too my portrait has been removed from above the desk. The space where it used to hang is darker than the surrounds. The desk and chair are the same and showing their age. I run my fingers over a scratch in the desk's surface. I remember making it – a slip of a knife. I remember it becoming dark with age. I turn to face the Marshal who just now appears in the door.

'You seem to know your way around.'

'Apparently so.'

Momentarily I feel as if I am back in my post and this man is the supplicant, instead of me. I find myself moving to the chair behind the desk but stop. I stand to one side and let the Marshal pass. He asks me to sit.

'How may I help?' The Marshal sits behind the desk, facing me.

'You no doubt know who I am,' I begin. 'You no doubt know that according to the terms of my sentence I am not allowed to return to the settlement on pain of death. Nonetheless I have returned. You must be wondering why I have done so, why I have flouted the terms of my sentence.'

I pause but the Marshal says nothing.

'I am surprised, I have to say, at the lack of urgency shown by you at my presence, at Andalus's presence indeed. I am surprised I am being left alone and not arrested. It is an agreeable turn of events in some ways but one which I would like to understand. We have things to clear up here. Firstly, you should be aware of the reasons for my presence since I believe as Marshal you have a duty to react to them. That is my major concern, as it has always been. Secondly, I would like to understand what this means. Why has the policy of the town been to ignore me, to pretend they don't remember, for this must be what is going on? Perhaps it is not my concern. I am, after all, no longer of this place. Nonetheless I would like to understand what it means. Will I be forced to leave again? Will I face execution? Will I have to serve time in prison within the colony? I hope for leniency, given the dangers I have faced bringing Andalus here, bringing him to your notice. Thirdly, I would like to talk about the events of the past, about what we did.'

He interrupts me. 'Who is this man you have brought to us?'

'You must know who he is. Andalus, the General of Axum, the one who brought near destruction on our people, as we did on his. The one I fought, the one with whom I concluded a peace.'

'I have not seen Andalus.' This time he changes his pronunciation.

'He appears to be traumatised. He is certainly not the same man who led Axum. Something has happened and I believe we need to try to discover what it is. In the time since I found him he has not spoken, has not said a word. He is docile. Quite tame. Much like a dog, you might say. He does what you tell him. Every now and then I can see a glimmer in his eyes of who he used to be. There was an instance on the island when I was chopping wood. He came up behind me, like a ghost, and the expression in his eyes … I did not trust him for a while after that but he seems harmless.'

'You were on an island?'

'Yes.' I look at him unblinking. 'I survived.'

'Tell me about this island.'

I contain my irritation at the changing of the subject and decide to humour him. 'My calculations told me I was on the very edge of our territories as agreed with Axum. Any further and I would have been in violation of the Treaty and you could have been back at war. Banished by the town I saved, for carrying out what was necessary to save them, only to initiate war as a result of my banishment. You did not think of that possibility when you gave me a raft and a few provisions.'

'I gave you a raft?'

I make a point of maintaining my patience. 'Not you personally, though I'm sure you had some role in the whole proceeding. Not you but your office, specifically the man who occupied that seat before you, Marshal Abel.'

'Abel?'

'Yes, Abel. You are not going to tell me you have forgotten him as well.'

The Marshal smiles and looks down at his desk. 'So, tell me about the island.'

Again I feel this is a waste of time but it is dawning on me that my people have lost a sense of urgency. Things have slowed down. I begin: 'The island is a dead place or to be accurate, a dying place. It is like a body lying face down in a pool of muddy water, slowly sinking, slowly drowning.' I stop myself.

'The island I have documented well. I have brought my notes with me.' I tap the bag that I hold. 'My intention was to hand over the notes to the town's geographer. Though the island is disappearing there is knowledge there and since we have lost such a lot, a little is valuable.'

The Marshal holds up his hand to stop me opening the bag. 'That can wait,' he says.

I fix him with a stare. 'You are right. There is little of interest on the island. The island is not the story here, or at least not the main story. What is of interest is Andalus and what is to be done with him.'

'Still, humour me. How long were you on the island and how did you come to return to us?'

'Ten years. I arrived there about three weeks after being sent away from here. It was the first dry land I had seen. Relatively dry at least. I set up camp. I found water. I caught fish. I made fire from peat and from wood found in a small forest. I harvested grains and tubers. I caught seagulls every now and then. They were mostly dead already. I worked out how long the island would last, how quickly it was slipping into the water. I noted the rates at which food stocks dwindled – the fish, the birds – and worked out how long my fuel sources would last. I made annotations on the types of fish I caught, the varieties of grains I found, the earth, the rocks. I did not plant more because I did not need more. My life I realised would run out with the island's. That was how it was for all the time I was there.

'One day Andalus washed ashore. There he was, a large white being stranded on my shore. It took me a while to recognise him but eventually I did. He showed no signs of recognising me. In fact he showed no signs of noticing what was around him at all.

'I began to realise what his presence might mean and decided I should do what was right and face death by bringing him to your attention. And here I am.'

'And here you are.' He pauses, then asks, 'And how long do you plan to stay?'

I shake my head. 'There are still questions, things to be done.' I lean in towards the Marshal. 'What have you done with Marshal Abel? What have you done with his lover, Tora?'

'Tora?'

'My lover, before I left.'

'You think I should know you?'

'If you don't, you are a simpleton.'

His expression changes. 'You are a guest in this town. Do not forget.'

'A guest you don't know what to do with. You have choices: give him the best room, or, try to ignore him in the hope that he will go away, or, take him outside into the orange groves, set on him, slit his throat, bury him so no one can see.'

'We will not kill you. We are a good people, a forward-looking people.' With that the Marshal leans back in his chair, folds his arms behind his head and looks up at the ceiling. He speaks again. 'You were here last night.'

This throws me slightly. 'How did you know it was me?'

'Your footprints were all over the place.'

'How did you know they were mine?'

The Marshal shrugs. 'Who else?'

'The door was open.'

He says nothing.

'I walked into the hall. I have seen what you've done.'

'What have I done?'

'You have erased my name from the wall of names.'

'Erased, you say?'

'Erased. Perhaps a joke. Perhaps some ill-advised conception of public good.'

'Explain?'

'Someone, you, the real Marshal, someone, not liking what we did, chose to eliminate traces of the person most closely associated with the error. Error, as they saw it.'

'What error is that?'

I hesitate, wondering if he is being deliberately obtuse, or is admitting that he too sees the merits of what we did. 'The error, as some like to call it, of eliminating the weak, of following the policy that killed some yet saved so many. The policy designed to fix our world, broken in an original sin. The policy that some called a cull.'

The Marshal stares at me for a few moments. 'Why were you here?'

'Why was I here? I was passing. The door was open. I was curious. I wanted to see my old rooms again. I wanted to see my name on the list.'

'And you were disappointed when you did not see your name?'

'Of course. You do not erase history simply because you do not approve, simply because you wish you had another and this is clearly what has happened here.'

'By removing names from a wall?'

'It's emblematic. The removal of the names stands in the stead of something greater, something darker.'

'You think we should keep telling ourselves the stories that frighten us?'

I think I might be on the verge of extracting a confession from the Marshal.

'Why should you be afraid of it? The past has as much power over you as you allow it. Punish if you like. Crucify if you must. Burn the guilty and throw their ashes to the wind, blacken their names and cast out their families. Do not sweep under the carpet. Avenge guilt and move on. Even the guilty deserve to be remembered, deserve the status of being guilty.' Too much, I tell myself.

The Marshal betrays no emotion. After a while he looks down at the table and says, 'Let's go down to the hall then. Let's see if what you're saying has merit.' I want to remark that what I say has merit regardless of what is on the wall but I hold my tongue.

We do not talk again until we are in the Great Hall. I am about to point out the error when the Marshal says, 'Madara, Abel. Not a long line yet, though an auspicious one.'

I am surprised to say the least. 'The first is not the right name. You must know that. And you have an Abel there but no end date to his rule. Tell me, where is he, what has become of him? And why is your name not there? Are you not proud to be Marshal?'

He snaps at me. 'I have more important things to do than write my name on a wall. It will get done soon enough.'

'Regardless, Madara is still wrong.'

'What should be written on the wall?'

'I think you know the answer to that but I will indulge you,' I say. 'The first Marshal of Bran was Bran. Me, the man named for the settlement. The second Marshal was Abel, my second-in-command. He became Marshal when I was banished. You may very well be the third Marshal but I cannot say for sure.'

'You cannot say.'

'Cannot say whether you're the third, the fourth, the fifth. You know very well what I mean. The names on that list, if there are three, should be Bran, Abel, Jura. That is the error. The wrong names, the wrong number.'

The Marshal walks up to the wall, stands with his nose almost touching it, looking at the names. He puts his hand to them and rubs his fingertips over the gold lettering. 'You asked if I was proud. I am very proud to be Marshal of Bran and to follow such men. Madara then Abel, a man even greater than the first.' He pauses. 'On wood such as this you would have to be extremely careful sanding it if your alterations were not to stand out. Extremely careful. It has such a soft texture, is so finely grained that only an expert craftsman would be able to remove paint and then repaint without leaving any traces of his work. Come and have a look.'

I step closer.

'Do you see any marks?' He points to the name Madara. 'Do you see any difference in the wood?'

I have to admit I do not.

'Then,' he says, barely bothering to conceal his triumph, 'You have to concede that you are wrong.'

'You said yourself an expert craftsman could have done it.'

'You misunderstand. But, never mind.' He turns away from me, his back to the wall. 'You say you know a great deal about history but I am not sure you have learnt from it. Nevertheless it has been a pleasure talking with you. I enjoy the exchange of ideas. You must come again and we can continue our discussion. Of course you should announce yourself when you do and not walk around like a thief.' I cannot tell if he is serious or not. 'But for now you must go.' He walks off.

At the entrance to the hall he turns around, looks me in the eyes and says, 'Madara was our first ruler. In some ways a truly great man. He wrote our constitution. He saved us all from starvation. But he was brutal, too brutal. Perhaps a man of his time. Then that time ended and he could no longer be a man of his time. He had to go. He had to end. That is his story. Abel took over. His was the true vision, a vision that healed us and gave us stability and a sense of purpose, an identity we have come to cherish.'

I am too stunned to reply. I can only watch the Marshal leave. But then I shout, 'You cannot deny me forever, Jura. You will have to reckon with me in the end.'

I turn back to the wall, run my palm over the wood again. I walk out of the room, out of the building, out of the courtyard. As I go I look up at the window. Perhaps a shadow, a hand, a pale face. Perhaps nothing.

I have left without answers but I will be back. If I can't get answers from the Marshal, I will find them myself. I will find proof of what is being done here. I will find Abel and Tora.

I walk quickly to Abel's house again. I knock hard at the door, place my ear to the wood and listen intently. There is nothing. Once more I knock and listen.

After a few moments I tiptoe away from the door to the window. I cannot see through it. The sun shines brightly on the pane and blinds me. I place my face against the glass. At first I can see nothing. One by one objects become visible: the stone floor, a chair, a table, a chest against a wall. On the chest a jug and basin. At the far end of the room a passageway deeper into the house. The chair has been knocked over. Peering to my left I can make out where the door should be but cannot see it as it is just behind a wall that juts out, blocking my vision. I imagine someone standing there, waiting for me to leave. I press further into the glass, using my hands placed around my face to block out the glare of the sun. The floor is covered in a grey film of dust. It is thin, just a few days old.

It is obvious to me by now that I will get no easy answers. Few people look at me in the streets. One, the judge, has run away from me. The two, three hundred people whose names I knew have vanished. A Marshal who is plainly not a leader of men. A woman who pretends not to know me or her predecessor, pretends reluctantly perhaps, out of duty, obligation. That I do not know.

They seem to be trying to forget. That would be a tragedy. It is only the weak who forget their past. If you kill a man who has no memory of his place in the world, none of the ties that bind him to his community, can you say you have really killed a man at all? What is a man but his past and his companions? There would be no loss felt. With peoples too. Only a weak people forgets its past, a nation that can be wiped out and restarted without anyone noticing. In place of a history, only a silence with no one to hear it. A pathetic people and if that is what they choose then they deserve what comes to them.

My people have been given a history by war. They were trimmed down the better to face an inhospitable world. That is the history of these people. The man running away, the one who knocked me over, the people sitting in the kitchens ignoring me, the Marshal, Elba, they should not forget where they came from. Born of hunger and necessity they are the survivors, they are the ones that had to bear the burden of the future, a future that the weak impinged upon. Do they feel guilt? That is not their burden. There is no question of guilt anywhere in this land, there has been no guilt since we first started fighting, since we first started slitting each other's throats in a frantic bid to survive. These people do not have the imagination to feel guilt. They do not have the right to feel it.

Is it simply a case of forcing them into remembrance, forced memory? Is it simply a case of gathering enough proof so they cannot deny me, until they take a breath and pluck up the courage to stare the past – and me – in the face?

Duty is what they should feel. Not guilt but duty. They have a duty as the last representatives of a once-dominant species to remember that which came before. For we have nothing else.

It is disappointing to me what they seem to have become. Shadows. Ghosts. Have I created them like this? Have I scared them into hiding in the corners like children? No. I too am the product of a shattered world. But I showed how it can be mended, how it can be pulled together piece by bloody piece.

I see them approach from afar, one much taller than the other. Elba and Amhara. They have already seen me. I stop and wait for them to come closer. Amhara wears a red coat. Again I am reminded of when I first saw her. I have the same feeling now I had then.

'Morning,' Elba says.

'Hello Elba. Hello Amhara.' The girl looks at the ground.

Elba continues, 'I am sorry if I was abrupt last night.'

I shake my head.

'Would you like to try again?' she asks.

'Try calling again?'

'No. Well, yes. I am trying to invite you to dinner again,' she says. 'Tonight?'

'I would like that,' I reply.

'Good.' She does not say goodbye but turns and is off. I watch them make their way down the street. At the corner, Amhara turns to look at me. I wave at her. She does not wave back.

There is a limit to what I can do during daylight but there are at least two things. I can start knocking on doors, trying to find someone who I recognise or someone who will talk to me. I can also head back into the orange groves and to the clearing in the middle of it, the place where we hanged the weak.

Of course there is the risk that they will shut the gates when I am out and not allow me back in but I will have to take that risk. I want to find evidence of my work. Some documents were stored in a hut on the site and if they are still there might help my case.

On my way to the gates I see Andalus in the distance. I am annoyed at his wanderings but I cannot keep him close, in my vision, all the time and still pursue the truth.

I am not used to limitations. On the island the limits were only of my choosing.

I call to him but he is too far off. He is a grey shape in the distance, a shape broken up by the heat mirage. I am reminded of the first morning at the town gates. I run to catch up with him. He turns a corner and is gone. I beat the wall of a house with my fist. The door to the house opens. It opens towards me. I can see a man's shadow between gap and frame. I wait for him to show his face. He does not come out. The door begins to close. I shout and run towards it but I am too late.

I walk through the trees, through the dappled, green light, dragging my hands through the grass and along the bark of the trees. I walk through the light, the sun cooled by the shade of the citrus leaves. I lift my hands to my face. I smell the acids, the oils. I realise, in some ways I am entranced by my old town, by what it has become. Entranced and frustrated. Can one give oneself over to love completely that which is not perfect, that which is wrong? I want to say yes. Part of me wants to yield to the town. I know I could slip back into its embrace, yield myself to the caresses of Elba, forget about Abel, about Tora, about my part in all this. I could raise the girl, perhaps start a family of my own. Begin over. Though that may not be possible. Elba has reached the age where it would be dangerous for her to give birth. A surrogate family then. Something not perfect, something incomplete, impure. Too far on in history for purity.

And too many questions. Too many things left unfinished for there to be satisfaction in a quiet life.

Some of the fruit is so low I have to duck as I walk under the branches. In places the thick foliage makes it dark. I walk deep into the orchard seeing no one. There is no sound other than my footsteps. I am amazed at the abundance of fruit. Some of it is overripe, as if they have more than enough and could not be bothered to pick it. In my day we harvested what we could and kept watch over it to prevent theft. But there is no one here.

I break through the trees suddenly and find myself in a sun-filled clearing. Trees give way to long green grass, and in the centre, quite incongruous for our settlement, a stone hut, about four by four metres. Though the surrounds have changed much, somehow I have found my way here easily. All those years ago there were just a few trees. Trees that were sturdier than orange trees. A few of these are still standing, I notice, still standing in a circle around the hut.

I kept this place fenced off. It was a mile from the settlement gates, not quite out of sight. I have been walking over the graves for the last hundred metres. We used to bury them here, here where they died. We started at the hut and buried them in circles, spiralling away from the centre as we had to bury more and more.

We buried them in shallow graves with their faces pointing skywards. That way, some believed, they could rise again to join a better world, a world made possible by their passing. Often several bodies to a grave. We buried them but our burial was not a forgetting, was not meant to be a forgetting. I am angry that the markers seem to have been removed. We were careful to mark the graves with a small pile of stones. But they have not been moved. I scuff the grass with my foot and disturb a pile. Not moved, just buried and forgotten. At least they are still here but they should not be overgrown like this. If there was so much fuss about what we did to these people, why then have they not been remembered? This is not remembrance, leaving the graves to be overgrown by grass and fruit trees. I have a vision of a corpse in the earth. The roots of an orange tree pierce the earth, pierce the bag, pierce the flesh of man. The fruit of the trees that feed the town nourished by the death of our ancestors.

On the other hand, better a fruit orchard and undisturbed peace than dry ground, a baking sun and a few small stones as a monument in a bleak landscape.

I have brought the island stone with me. I remove it from my bag and look around the clearing for somewhere to put it. There is no obvious place. It seems a hollow gesture but I place the stone on the ground before me. It is darker than the others I have disturbed. I straighten up and take a deep breath. I am left feeling flat.

I walk up to the hut. The one window is boarded up though not entirely. Two planks form an x. The door has been nailed shut. I peer in. It takes a few moments for my eyes to adjust to the gloom. There is not much to see. At first glance it seems everything has been removed. But not everything. A white shape lies sprawled across the table inside. I jerk back. The shape of a head, two lumps at the end for feet, an arm hanging down at one side. It does not move. I know of course it is not a body. But the sight of it brought it back. Real enough. An imagined body standing in place of hundreds before it. It fills the space of the dead.

I kick the door in. I approach the shape slowly, walking through dust. There are dust motes in the air like flies. They shimmer in the shaft of light coming through the doorway. I walk up to it, reach out my hand, touch it. It gives in easily when I touch it. It is one of the bags we stored people in before burial. For a moment I think I will see Tora's mother when I tear it open, as if she had died yesterday, but all I see inside are more of the bags. They seem to have been arranged to look like a corpse. Why I don't know. I pull them out one by one. More dust. There is a scuttling from behind me. I wheel around sharply but see nothing. At the door I squint against the light. I can see no one. 'Who's there?' I shout. No answer. I walk around the hut to the other side but there is nothing and I hear no more sounds. A rabbit, I assume. I re-enter the hut and dismantle the pretend corpse. I find myself sneezing from the dust. The noise startles me again.

I look around the room. Everything has been removed, except for the table and the bags. There was never much call for equipment. A chair, a table, a small platform, a cabinet, some rope, a stove for heating food for the guards, knives, twine, bags. That was it.

The cabinet, which used to contain records, is gone.

I walk to the far wall. I raise my hand to it. I run my fingers over the marks. We made a small mark with a stone on the wall of the hut.

The seventh line we drew crossed the previous six. At the end of fifty-two of these we started a new row. Why we measured the dead in this way, the way we measured time, I cannot recall. Did each death mean another day's life granted to the settlement? Perhaps. But it is a sign of respect too. A mark, inscribed in stone, will never die.

I step back. The marks reach across the wall and from floor to ceiling. I am surrounded by them. Suffocated.

I know how many of them there are. I do not have to count. There are nine hundred and seventeen scratches on the wall.

I can remember the name behind the first mark, the name behind the last, some in between. I tried on the island to remember more. I lay on my bed each night and went over the names, glancing over at the cave wall. I willed myself to remember more. After a while I'd force myself to stop by listening only to the wind, the waves. I did not think about Bran, about Tora, Abel, about my banishment. Just the names. Only the names. The faces, mostly blank, nameless, pushed against the rock of my cave, against the wall of days, straining to get through. I shut my eyes to keep them out.

When Tora came to me after I hanged her mother I held her close. I hugged her and felt my heart leap. But then I looked at my hands on her back. I remembered the blood, the blood of her mother on my hands, hands separated from Tora's skin by just a thin dress. I let go of her with that hand, held on tighter with the other. I think though, it seemed as if I wanted to let her go. I did not. I wanted to carry on holding her. On and on. She looked hurt. I could not explain. She broke my grip, brushed past me and went to pour herself a glass of water.

For each one of the nine hundred and seventeen I gave to myself the task of pronouncing the c-grade. I took this on myself. For each

I pronounced death. Some cried. Some tried to attack me. Most were too feeble. I have been cursed a thousand times.

I close the door and go outside and again walk round the back of the hut. It is overgrown, the trees unpruned. My feet bury themselves in rotting fruit, weeds, dead branches. Like mud. I kick at it. My boots dislodge something hard. I bend down to pick it up. It is a few centimetres long and caked in brown earth. It is not wood, it is much too hard for that. I wipe off some of the earth. I can see the pores now. It is bone, of that I'm sure. From what I do not know. It could be anything: dog, human. I kick away more of the earth and get down to my hands and knees and dig a little deeper. The digging is tough and I can only go a short way down, barely scratching the surface. With better implements I could, I know, uncover whole skeletons. But what would that prove? Without names it proves nothing. But I do find another. I pull it out. It is from the leg of a human. I wrench it out of the earth, stones and leaves scattering as I do. I stand there with it. I stand there with the bone of a man's leg in my hand and I tilt my head back and my eyes shut against the light.

There are patterns on my eyelids made by the light. I open and close them, again and again, hoping the shapes will go away. They return brighter and brighter. I begin to see their faces. Their faces start to come back. I am surrounded by trees. From each branch hangs a corpse. Ants crawl over their skin. The corpses stretch back into the grove, back far into the dark of the orchard. The black bodies sway gently in the breeze. I can hear the ropes creak.

It is late afternoon when I get back to the town. I make my way to the shelter. Andalus has re-appeared. He is dozing in the late sun, leaning against a wall. I sit next to him, our shoulders touching. He wakes but does not move. I tilt my head towards him. In a way his bulk is comforting. Real. I pat him on the hand. 'Andalus,' I say. 'Andalus. I am getting nowhere. I came here to save us but I am getting nowhere.'

He does not answer. He has his arms resting on his legs. An image crosses my mind. I saw this picture as a child. I found it in a ruin my group came across as we moved south. In the picture were creatures shaped like men but with bigger jaws and heavier foreheads. They were covered in black hair and standing in a forest of the lushest green. To my child's mind they were both frightening and alluring. If I think back, perhaps that is what helped make me more curious about the past than others: a picture of strange beasts in a strange land. I showed it to no one. My parents had been dead a long time – I only ever had a vague idea of what they looked like – and I had few friends. But it was something I would not have shared even if things had been different. I kept it for years. One of the animals was sitting in exactly the same position as Andalus is now. How has he come to this? I am beginning to believe he is not simply traumatised by whatever happened to him in Axum but has lost his reason as well. The possibility has to exist that nothing happened to him. No big trauma, no big event, no mutiny, uprising or trial. Perhaps he lost his reason and simply wandered off one day never to return. Kept alive by the colony as an indication of humanity to a once-great ruler, one day he simply slipped his velvet shackles and sloped off. A not entirely unreasonable explanation.

I think again of another possibility. He is cleverer than I am. He spies me on an island, begins an act, an elaborate ruse. I bring him back, he worms his way into favour here and leads an army back across the seas and the plains to re-conquer Axum, take it back from the mutineers, from the third force, and impose law and order. He is biding his time, waiting for the right moment to speak. In the end his play will out.

I wonder how it would be if the situation was reversed. If I had been exiled, sailed unknowing into Axum territory, encountered Andalus alone on an island, what would I have done?

I continue: 'They are hiding from us, Andalus. Of that I am becoming convinced. What other explanation could there be? It has only been ten years. They have locked away Abel and Tora. Either that or Abel is directing it. His name is still on the wall. Anyone who knows me well remains out of sight while I wander the streets. While I am here their lives are in hiatus. The only people allowed on the street are children and the ones they know I won't know.'

I lean my head against the wall.

'Of course, I have no proof of this. It is merely a theory. And I don't understand why. Why not put an arrow through me and be done with it? Why not face me and say, "No, you are not allowed. Be gone." It seems weak. A mark of weakness.'

I look over to him. 'I need your help, Andalus. I will get to the truth. I will force it out of these people one way or the other. I will force them to acknowledge me, like I, like we in fact, forced them to face the truth of our situation all those years ago. But it will be quicker if you help.'

I turn to him. 'Don't you want to fix things? Don't you want an end to all this? To all the thoughts, all the ghosts, the hundreds of ghosts?'

And then he shakes his head. It is so slight I might have imagined it. I wait but there is no further movement.

'Is that your answer, Andalus? Is that your answer? No? Don't you feel anything?'

His head is pointed away from me now. It is still. Perhaps he was just moving to get away. Not answering. His eyes are closed. I pull his face towards me and they open. 'Did you give me an answer?'

His eyes have a vacant look. They remind me of the ocean we sailed across. Blue-grey. Lifeless. But somewhere in there, drowned perhaps, a sapphire city, a memorial to a great man, a memory, a history.

When I arrive at Elba's later, Amhara opens the door. Before I can say anything she has run off leaving me to enter the flat on my own.

'Hello?'

'In here. In the kitchen.'

Elba is bent over a small stove.

'I thought all those had long since been confiscated,' I say, nodding in the direction of the stove.

She laughs. 'No. We are allowed now.'

'So you do acknowledge things have changed,' I say.

She looks around, a puzzled expression on her face. 'Of course. Things change all the time.' It is as if she is challenging me.

There is a smell in the kitchen that makes my stomach rumble. I have not eaten all day. Amhara rushes in and goes straight to her mother, whispering in her ear.

Elba turns around. 'My daughter would like you to tell her a story.' She smiles apologetically. Amhara turns sharply and looks angrily at her mother. It is only momentarily though and I might be mistaken. I decide to ignore it.

'A story? Let me think. Would you like to hear more about the island?'

She nods her head but does not look at me.

'Well then,' I sit down at the table. 'I lived in a cave on the island. It rained all the time. Not like here. I had not seen the sun for ten years, other than as a white disc through clouds. It was a dull world: grey, brown, pale green. These are not the colours of life. I might have given you the impression last time that the island was paradise. It was not. It was a hard life. Not unbearable certainly. But not to feel the sun on your skin for ten years, only the rain, is not a good way to live. And the silence. I would see things.' I stop abruptly. I had not meant to say that.

'Who else was there?' asks the child.

'Who else? No one. No one else was there. It was just me. Me, the birds, the fish, the worms.'

'What did you see?'

I look hard at her, then at Elba. 'I saw people. I mean, I know they weren't actually there but if you're alone for a long time you start to imagine things. And part of me wanted them to be there, wanted them to come back.'

'Did you miss your friends?'

I am glad she has slightly misunderstood. 'There was a woman,' I glance over at Elba. 'There was a woman I missed. I hope she missed me a little. There was another man. He was once a friend of mine. I did not miss him much.'

'Why not?'

'He was the one who sent me away, who conspired with the towns-people to have me removed from power and banished to the edges of Bran.'

'Why did he do that?'

I pause. 'People felt a change was needed. I was no longer needed.'

Amhara thinks for a while. 'So you were alone.'

'Yes. But then one day I found someone. I was walking along the coast and I spied him from some distance off lying on the sand. He had been washed up. I nursed him back to health gave him food and shelter.'

'Where is he now?'

'I brought him back to Bran. He is a very important man. I knew I had to bring him back. Our future might depend on it. I left him where I am staying. He is not very talkative.' I say this with a smile.

'Why not?'

'I don't know. I suppose he had some kind of shock and is unable to speak for now. It happens sometimes. In war people see things they don't like. It shocks them. Sometimes they become silent. I have seen it many times.'

'Has it happened to you?'

'No. I have been lucky.'

Her face down, she seems to be pondering what I have said.

'How is he your friend if he doesn't speak? He must speak for you to know him.'

'That is a good question. I knew him years ago, years before he arrived on the island. His name is Andalus, General of Axum, a very powerful man. Years ago I was very powerful here too. You would have been born soon after I left and stopped being Marshal of this settlement. Between us we brought peace. We had known long years of war. But we ended it because we could see that it was of no use. We ended the senseless deaths of thousands of young people.'

I look at Elba to see if I am going too far but she has her back to me and does not turn around.

'This was more than twenty years ago, twenty-two years in fact since I last saw him. Our two groups were at peace. We had promised to take care of our own and never to go to the other's territory. Never. So I thought I would not see him again. And then he turns up on the island. It got me thinking.'

The girl asks, 'What did you think?'

'I began to wonder if we were about to go to war again. Don't you think it's strange that my friend should turn up in Bran territory after promising that neither he nor his kind would ever come near us again?'

At this point Elba turns around and says, 'That's enough stories.'

Amhara says, 'I would like to hear more.' She looks at Elba, who gives in easily.

'Alright. A bit longer,' she says.

I continue, 'There was another reason I came back.'

'What was that?'

'He and I were powerful men, with ideas that suited the time. Some didn't like them, said the ideas were barbaric. They tried to stop us.'

'Were they right?'

I don't answer. Instead I say, 'I've come back to try and fix things.' I look at her mother when I say this.

Elba puts down the plate she was holding. 'She's too young, Bran. Amhara, no more questions.'

The child stares at me from across the table, ignoring her mother. After a few moments she says, 'I would like to see your friend.'

'Your mother has seen him,' I say.

'Have I?' She seems to forget her instructions to Amhara.

'Yes. At the kitchens. I came in with him.'

Elba furrows her brow. 'I don't remember him, sorry.'

'He was sitting opposite me. You have also seen me with him in the town.'

She shakes her head. 'I am sorry.'

I am surprised. He is not a forgettable sight.

Elba turns to Amhara and says, 'Now it is bedtime. Say goodnight.'

The girl ignores her. She looks at me and says, 'She's not my mother, you know.'

Elba drops a pan and rounds on her. 'You are not to say that.' Her voice is a breathless whisper. 'What did we say?'

Amhara looks at the table. She has a scowl on her face. 'Well, you're not. You just pretend to be.'

'Off you go! Goodnight.'

Amhara walks away without a word.

I smile apologetically at Elba. For a moment I do not know what to say. I want to ask about what Amhara said, but Elba speaks first. 'The child is overly imaginative. I wish you wouldn't go putting ideas into her head. The story of Andalus and you is a good one, very creative, but should not be told to a little girl.'

'It is not a story, Elba. It needs to be told. And people need to listen. And I don't believe someone can be overly imaginative. Without ideas, visions, we may as well be dogs.' I surprise myself with this outburst. Elba says nothing.

I cede, 'But yes, perhaps a story of impending war is not one to be told to a child before bed.'

She nods her head. 'I am going to dish up. I have some wine,' inclining her head in the direction of a cupboard. 'Would you pour some?'

We do not talk much after that and the silences are slightly uncomfortable. I want to talk about Amhara's comments, about Elba not remembering Andalus, but I take care to avoid making her angry. Towards the end of the evening though, I tell her about my earlier talk with the Marshal. I notice she does not look at me or pass comment throughout. 'What do you think?' I ask eventually.

She looks straight at me. 'I think the Marshal is right. And I don't think you should concern yourself with these stories anymore.'

This takes me aback. 'Right? Right about what?'

'Just right. Right about everything. Our first Marshal was Madara. A great man, albeit a violent one. He was a saviour to some, a beast to others. But whatever he was, he is dead to us. We have moved on. You should not concern yourself with altering names.'

I do not know what she means. 'No. You are incorrect. We have to acknowledge these alterations. We have to find the persons responsible. I can see that the torpor of life here means that people seem to accept whatever stories they are told because not to would be too much trouble.' I have been banging my fork on the table. She covers my hand with hers and holds a finger to her lips.

'You'll wake the child.'

I nod. 'I apologise. But Madara is a fiction, a made-up person, a character in a play.'

Elba gets up, just as she did last night and goes to stand by the window. 'Have you heard of the legend of Bran? You must have since your name is Bran. We tend to know things that are close to us.'

'I have.'

'Then you will know Bran too was once a great king. He ruled in a time when no one can remember, when no one can remember having been told of. He ruled a kingdom located somewhere in the east. Somewhere. Head east and as soon as you see the flowing rivers, soaring mountains and fruit falling off trees, you will know you are there. They say strange creatures live there.'

She pauses. 'He came to power at a dangerous time for his people. They were weak. But he defeated all who came before him. He went looking for neighbours to destroy. He protected his people, made them strong, made them rulers of all others. Then one day he died. He was shot in the back by one of his own marksmen. An accident. They pulled the arrow out but that was what killed him. He bled to death and his blood soaked into the ground of his beloved land.'

She talks as if reciting something memorised.

'The people were frightened. Their saviour was gone. They took a knife and cut off his head. They took it to the edge of the kingdom, the shoreline. They placed it on a stake facing out to sea. The glare was so terrible, so frightening, it warned off all invaders. His country was never conquered and it became a peaceful place without him, with just the memory of him.'

'Are you saying that is what has happened to me?'

Elba scoffs. 'No. It is just a story. Something that happened. That might have happened.'

I go over to join her at the window. I hesitate, then put my hand on her shoulder. To my surprise she tilts her head, so her cheek is resting on my fingers.

'What did she mean?'

'Who?'

'Amhara. What did she mean when she said you weren't her mother?'

She stiffens beneath my touch.

'She is approaching a difficult age.'

'Still, what did she mean?' I am aware I risk antagonising the only person who has taken an interest in me but the truth is more important.

Elba pulls away and turns to face me. 'She meant nothing. What do you mean asking such a question?'

'Who is the father?'

'I told you.'

'Is she mine?'

Elba hesitates, then laughs. She steps back. She laughs again. It is a shallow laugh.

I continue. 'She isn't your daughter, is she?'

The smile disappears.

'She's Tora's daughter. When I first arrived I noticed it but I've only just realised I did. I saw Tora in her. I see myself in her too.'

Elba's eyes flicker. Her lips move but she says nothing. She simply stares.

I reach out and take hold of her arms. 'Tell me what is going on. Tell me why no one claims to recognise me. Tell me why no one will acknowledge me.' I am bending slightly, as if about to kneel.

'Tell me what game is being played. Why are you all pretending not to know me?'

She does not answer.

'I will not let this go. I could slip back into life here, settle down, maybe even with you.' She does not look up. 'But I cannot do that yet. I mean to find out what has happened to this town since I left, what has happened to Abel, to Tora. It is for your good. Our good. How can you progress if you do not remember?'

She looks at me now, more composed. 'Why do you presume to

know what is in our best interests? You turn up here out of the blue, the dust of the mountains on your coat, a strange old-fashioned way of talking and you claim to have been Marshal here, to have started this settlement even. You have all these stories. I am not afraid of you. I put your eccentricities down to, well, an eccentric nature, which, it is true, this town lacks. We have solid burghers who go about their business but no one who loves telling stories. That is what I like about you. But you go on so. Can you not admit defeat, say you are wrong, say that during these ten years you say you were away, something happened to you that you cannot remember, something that changed who you are? You say you were banished but is it not possible you are simply a sailor who got lost, who came close to drowning in a shipwreck and when he woke up, though sane in every other way, believed that he was once a warrior, once a great man, once a killer?' She stops, slightly out of breath.

'Bran – you even have a name that may as well be made up. The same as the town. Are you a foundling? Perhaps you were brought here, devoid of all memories and stories, kept to the shadows and waited until a story weaved its way into you, until you knew who you were. Bran, the townsman. Man of the town. You say we are the ones deliberately forgetting you, wiping you out but can you really be sure it is not you who is making all this up? Are you certain the story you tell is true?'

'Now you are being ridiculous,' I say.

'Yes. Perhaps.' She pauses. 'But you cannot reasonably explain why a whole town would have conspired to cover up the existence of two men, a woman and an entire history.'

'I cannot explain yet why you have chosen this path. That is why I would like your help.'

'What answer do you want, Bran? What answer is there to give? You can never know us again.' She closes her eyes for a second, as if she has said something wrong.

'You said again. You do know me.'

'That is not what I meant. I do not know you.'

'I am Bran, your first Marshal.'

'I do not know you.'

'I am Bran.'

She shakes her head. 'No.'

I give her a push when I loosen my grip and turn away.

'Perhaps you should go.'

I walk out the door. I do not look back.

I make my way to Abel's house. I walk through the dark streets. There are few lights on. It is later than I thought. Moonlight makes shadows from the rooftops. Something moves on the edge of one. I look up quickly. I can see nothing. I turn full circle. Still nothing. I think back to the island, the heads staring at me from the top of the cliffs.

When I look down I see him. A figure, I cannot see a face. He presses back into a doorway. I call out. I begin to run up to him. A door opens behind him and he is gone.

I hurl myself at the door. I beat on it with both my hands. I step back and kick.

Mouse people. They keep to the shadows. They run from that which they don't understand.

This time I have my knife. It slips in easily. I give it a twist and feel the metal give way. It is easily done. The lock is smooth. It is not one that hasn't been opened for ages. I step into Abel's house and wait for my eyes to adjust to the gloom. The dust is everywhere. The whole room is grey with it, made greyer by the moonlight.

I hear myself calling out, 'Hello?' I do not know whether I expect an answer.

As I become more used to the dark I begin to make out objects, objects I recognise. There on the wall hangs a scabbard that belonged to Abel. I presented it to him after a battle in which he distinguished himself. Behind enemy lines, he led a small party of soldiers back to safety, capturing a watch post along the way. A most noble act in a time when one more defeat could have meant the end for us. I remember him accepting it. He was unsmiling. He looked at me as I handed it over. The expression in his eyes was almost hostile but more likely to have been determination. He was not one for smiles at the best of times.

I sense something has happened in this room. Things are out of place. A drawer is open. Abel was a very ordered man. It was why we worked well together. We were similar in that way. Nothing escaped his attention. For this to be Abel's house something must have happened. It is a mess. But it is Abel's house. With Abel's belongings.

There on the table a ledger of the type I had produced. I open it. It is blank save for the inscription, 'Property of Bran. To be returned to the office of the Marshal of Bran on demand.' I had asked for that inscription. It meant little in real terms but it was one of the building blocks of the settlement, one of the ways we clawed back the rule of law. As a gesture it meant everything. I close the cover. My fingers leave marks in the dust. I regret the absence of a date in the ledger, which would have given some clue as to the time of Abel's disappearance and the absence of any handwriting, either mine or Abel's, which would have helped prove my story.

I go into the kitchen. Here the cupboards are bare, the room empty save for a small table and the chair lying on its side. The bedroom leads off the kitchen. Inside it is almost completely black, the one window with blinds drawn. The only light comes from cracks between the planks. There is a wooden bed frame in the middle of the room and a chest at the foot of the bed. I open the lid. Inside, scrunched in a corner, is a jacket. My heart quickens. I shake it out. It is a military jacket. The insignia have been stripped off but from the number of tears I can tell it belonged to my deputy. I can picture it as it used to be. I look at the front pocket for the name. That too has been ripped off.

The bed is unmade. The sheets are crumpled. I lift them up, shake them out. I hold a blanket to my face. I can smell her. I breathe deeply. It smells of her. Like the soap on her hands. Like her hair. I lie down.

I sleep as if drugged. When I wake it is getting light. I take the jacket and walk through to the kitchen. There on the floor something catches my eye. Something half hidden under the dresser. A piece of paper folded in half. I open it.

And this is her.

Not just a smell, a scent, something a ghost might leave behind. It is her handwriting. Though it has been ten years I can tell. I know her. It reads – there are only a few words – 'Dear Bran, You should understand.' That line has been crossed out. It continues: 'There is a chasm between what we have been and what we want to be.'

I turn it over. There is nothing else. It ends there.

I stand and read it again. And again. Each time the words form the same sentences. Each time they end too soon.

I leave the house, emerging into early morning sunlight and close the door behind me. I do not attempt to lock it.

10

I walk over to the Marshal's office. There is a man at the top of the alleyway I see when I leave the shelter. He is gone by the time I reach the road. I am being kept under surveillance.

I do not knock. Instead I turn the handle. The door is open. I walk up the stairs to the Marshal's office.

He is sitting at his desk. He looks up as I enter. He does not look surprised to see me.

I sit down in the chair opposite him. I become aware of another man in the room. He sits in the corner behind my right shoulder. I turn around. Though I did not get a good look at him I think it is the man who knocked me over when I ran after the judge. He does not meet my gaze.

'What do you want, Bran?' the Marshal begins.

'Good morning,' I say. I wait for him.

Eventually he returns my greeting.

'I do not pretend to understand your treatment of me but it seems you may need some time to adjust, to ponder. I am a patient man but I require some answers from you. Though you might not think I have rights here anymore I believe I do. I have a right to be concerned that my people are losing their way.'

The Marshal leans back in his chair but does not respond.

'I have three questions for you. First, I would like to know the whereabouts of Abel, the second Marshal of Bran, the one who took over when I left, as well as the whereabouts of Tora. She was the woman who helped work out our meal plan. They might be found together if that helps though I suspect you might know that. I suspect you know very well where they are.'

Still nothing from him.

'Second, I demand to know why this elaborate charade. Why do you all pretend not to know me? Not to see me? Why do you all pretend to be someone else? You, for instance. You are no Marshal. You are not a leader of men. You act the part but Marshal is not in your essence. You are not a Marshal at your core.'

I pause. After a few seconds he asks, 'You mentioned three things?'

'Yes.' My tone alters. This is not as easy for me. 'I want something from you. It is less a question than a request.' I pause again.

'I found a man on my island. This man should not have been there. He means the balance has been disturbed. He means you have to reckon with the past again. He means that I am here now. That I am here before you demanding, asking, for you, for the settlement, to look again at me, to look at what I've done. And either kill me or set me free.'

'You are free.'

I look away from him, out the window. From here I can see the roofs of houses, the watchtowers on the gates and, beyond, blue in the distance, the mountains. Across those, across the plain, the ocean, lies the island, melting in the rain.

'What do you want from us, Bran?'

I turn back. I do not answer the question. Instead I say, 'I am gathering proof. Proof that what I say is true.'

'And what is that?'

'I have seen the judge. The one who sentenced me. I could see recognition in his eyes. Others too. You are keeping my friends and close acquaintances well hidden but I know a lot of people. Sooner or later they will out. This town is not a ghost town. People cannot stay in the shadows forever.'

'There must be more.'

'I have a letter addressed to me. I have a jacket that used to belong to Abel. I have found human remains. I extracted a confession from Elba.' This last point is an exaggeration and I watch the Marshal closely to see if he reacts.

'Elba?' he asks, his face still blank.

'That's right. I don't believe she is who she says she is. Just as you are not the real Marshal. Maybe she was a friend of Tora's. The child, who is not hers, seems to trust her, even if she does resent her a bit as well. But she is not who she says she is. And you. I have been trying to place you. You are familiar. You were a clerk in one of my offices, weren't you? An administrator.

Sometimes you used to put on plays in the town's courtyard to entertain us.'

While I am saying this I realise it is true. It has come back to me. At first I thought him a General but he is not. An insignificant man, until now, playing the part of a Marshal.

'You're having me followed.' He looks blank. 'In the orchard, last night, this morning.'

This time he does speak. 'You have an elaborate imagination. Who would want to follow you?'

'In the hut there was a pile of rags. It was shaped like a corpse. A body.'

'A pile of rags? Not a hollow man then? A rag man?' He sneers.

'Do you think it is appropriate in such a solemn place to leave effigies? The marks on the wall. Do they not make you cower? Do they not make you regret everything?' I stop myself.

'Better effigies, better make-believe, than bodies of flesh.'

'So you admit to knowing what went on there?'

'What went on there?'

'You know what we did. You are the inheritor of it. You are the children of it, the bastard of a father you're trying to forget.'

His face shows no emotion. 'And you? Are you my father?'

I wave away this question. 'What have you done with them?'

'With whom?'

'Where is everyone?'

He holds his arms out, palms upwards.

'What have you done with Abel and Tora? Are they orchestrating this or are they victims of it too? Have you had them killed? Imprisoned? Who is leading this?'

'You know who is leading this.' He speaks softly.

'Who?'

'I am. I am Marshal.'

'You are not.'

'I am Marshal of Bran. You are a wanderer. You have come in out of the wilderness. We wondered where you had come from. You came across the mountains. But before that? You speak of islands. You speak of a land where it rains incessantly. You speak of a man no one has seen. Is he made up? We look at you, stranger. You demand we remember you. You come here asking for, what was it, to be killed or set free? You abuse our hospitality with your unreasonable demands.'

I might have underestimated this man. He speaks slowly but firmly.

I stand up quickly and before the man in the corner can move I lift up Jura by his shirt. He is a large man but I am strong. 'You will reckon with me.'

The other man is up by now. I let go of Jura. I place both hands on the desk and lean in to him. 'You will reckon with me.'

I leave the room and close the door behind me.

It does not re-open. I walk down the corridor towards the room with the window behind which I believe I have seen someone watching me.

I reach the door. I place my ear to it. I can hear nothing. Or, I can hear something but I'm not sure what. When you hold a shell to your ear you hear the ocean. Do I hear breathing? I knock softly. Listen again. Still the breathing. I try the handle. The door is locked. I push against it. It is solid. I kneel and bend down. The gap between door and floor is small. Inside it is dark. But there are two darker shadows I can see. It is as if someone is standing on the other side, arm's distance away from me. The shadows do not move. It is silent in the corridor.

I whisper, 'Hello.'

No movement. No answer.

'Tora. It is me.'

I get to my feet. I place my palms on the door and lean in, press my cheek against it. It is warm. The temperature of blood.

'It is me. Bran. I have come back.'

There is nothing from the room.

I hear footsteps coming from down the corridor. I move further down and try the handle of the room next door. I am surprised when it opens. I close the door silently behind me. The key is in the lock and I turn it.

The footsteps stop, first outside the room next door, then outside my door. The handle turns slowly. Then they move off, further down the corridor.

I look around me. The walls are hidden for the most part. Against them leans a jumble of boxes, furniture and planks. It seems this room is used only for storage. I begin shifting some of the wood. I find a small wooden box. Shaking it produces a rattling sound. I open it and inside I find a child's toy, a man made of sticks, held together with twine. Or a woman perhaps, it is impossible to tell. I place it in my coat pocket to give to Amhara when next I see her. I pull back a large plank to see what's behind it. There is something leaning against the wall. It comes flooding back to me. I feel prickles at the back of my neck. The colours are faded, bits of paint are starting to flake off but there is no doubt what it is, who it is. It is me. I am in three-quarter profile but looking directly at the artist. The portrait that used to be behind my desk. The same painting. I look fiercer than I remember. I am in military uniform. There is black writing beneath the picture. I do not remember that either and I cannot make out what it says. This is it. This is the proof that will force them to confront me. I peer closely at the writing but still can't make it out.

I take the painting and go to the wall dividing the rooms. I knock on it. A shuffling. Indistinct. The sound a mouse might make.

'I will come for you.'

I don't know if I can be heard. I speak louder. 'I will come back for you. I promise.'

There is no one in the corridor. I walk back to the Marshal's office. The door is closed and locked. I see no one else in the building.

Outside though, the man from the office stands at one end of the courtyard. Though I have the portrait wrapped up and he cannot see what it is, there can be no doubt I have taken something. But he does not follow me. He watches me leave.

I see Amhara in the street. She wears the red tunic. She is some way ahead of me, darting in and out of sight, down side streets, up alleys. She stops and turns, looks in my direction. I hold my hand up to her. She is silhouetted red against a white building.

I go to her. As I get closer her companions emerge from the shadows, from the streets and walk up to me, float up to me. Their eyes are unblinking. They're close and they reach out to me. One grabs my arm, another pulls at my coat. They're silent, crowding around me. Amhara hasn't moved. She is taller than the others. 'Leave him,' she says. They look away and run off, disappearing again into the streets. Amhara stays, looks up at me. She takes my hand and squeezes. Her eyes like mine. The world is so much smaller in this moment. Everything stops. I open my mouth to speak but she turns and is gone. I remember the toy in my pocket too late.

I place the portrait in the shelter, covering it with tarpaulin. Andalus does not seem to notice what I'm carrying.

'I have proof,' I say to him.

He leans against the wooden frame of the shelter.

'Proof that everything is as I say it is. Proof that you and I are the bedrock on which this settlement has been built. Our settlements.'

I watch his eyes.

'And still you don't speak. I don't understand your game.

'Proof. But I want more. I am going to find more.'

I start at the first house after the town gate. I will work street by street, knocking on every door, waiting for an answer from every one. I will see if I recognise the person who opens the door. I will make sure they cannot close the door on me. If I don't recognise the person, to each I will ask the same questions: 'Where are Tora and Abel?' I will ask this, though I suspect I know the answer already. And: 'You remember me, don't you?' If they look me in the eye and say 'Yes' I will smile at them, thank them and leave. But they will not say that. They will not speak the truth.

There are about a thousand dwellings in the town. I do the sums in my head. One thousand houses, five minutes each. Fourteen or fifteen hours a day. It could take a week. And then not all the houses will be occupied when I reach them. I will have to come back again and again. But perhaps the very first house I come to will have an answer for me. The occupant of the first will stand to one side, invite me in. They will sit me down, take my hand, tell the truth.

Each house has in theory the same chance of being the true one. One in a thousand. But surely only the first house has those odds. The last house, the true house, has a one in one chance of being the right house. Does a house that is not the right one have any chance at all of being the right one? Would that I knew which is the last house.

Perhaps when I knock on one door an old crone will point down the road at a house and say, 'There, that is where you will find your answer.' A knock on that door elicits the response, 'No, not here but that house down there,' pointing to a third. And so on. With each step I move closer to and further away from the truth.

I sit on the steps of the first house for a few minutes. I hold my head in my hands. My forehead feels gritty, coated in sand, as if I am slowly being buried in the dust of the town.

The house behind me is silent. I knock on the door. Peer through the window. Try the handle. I pretend to leave and stand at the bottom of the steps, watching, listening.

Each house gives similar results. Sometimes there is movement inside. Sometimes there isn't. The doors never open.

When it is the house of someone I know I shout their name. I wait for the echo. I shout again.

I spend hours doing this. The sun goes down. I continue. For a while I do not notice my hunger.

I keep at it until the moon is high in the sky.

At the last house I try I hurl myself at the door. Again and again. I feel my skin grow raw. I open my mouth as if in a scream but I do not know if I make a sound.

Then I stop. I go back to the town hall.

But I cannot get in. I walk up to the Marshal's door in the moonlight. It is locked. I get out my knife to pick the lock. I hear a cough to my right. It is the man from the office. I turn to him. I begin to walk up to him, my knife in my fist. He takes a step back. I stop. I lower the knife. We look at each other for what seems like minutes.

It is not yet the time for that.

On my way out of the courtyard I look up at the window. Before I can see who it is, a figure draws the curtain. It sways for a bit and is then still.

11

I crawl out of the shelter in the morning and almost bump into the Marshal standing outside waiting for me. He is alone.

'Yes?' I say.

'Tonight. Tonight we will sort things out. You are to come to the town hall at sunset.'

I stare at him. 'What do you mean?'

'I mean, tonight we will know what will become of you.'

'And Andalus?'

'Andalus. Yes. I know what he is.'

'You know what he is.'

'He too is part of your game. Bring him too, if you can.'

'I am not the one playing a game.'

'Are you sure, Bran?'

With that he turns and walks away. As he rounds the corner, the other man appears. He stands in the middle of the road with his arms held behind him.

I go back in to the shelter. I speak to Andalus, 'I know you can talk. I need you to talk now.'

'I am beginning to think you are the cause of the hiatus. If I returned on my own they would have no hesitation in sending me on my way again, perhaps with an arrow between the shoulder blades. But as soon as they saw Bran and Andalus cresting the mountain they began to panic. They began to fear the resumption of war, the return of the past. And now they stay indoors and debate amongst themselves.

'This Marshal is not who he says he is. He used to be a minor official. I don't believe he is orchestrating this. I think he is standing in for someone else. He intends to communicate a decision about us tonight. They cannot keep up the deception forever. I am finding clues to support my story all the time. Left alone long enough I will have overwhelming evidence that all this,' I wave my arms in an arc, 'is an elaborate façade.

'But it would make it a lot easier if I had you to support me. Will you speak? Will you come with me? Tonight is when our fates will be sealed. I cannot see how this can go on for much longer. People will tire of staying indoors. Soon someone will set fire to this shelter, will come in the night armed with knives if only to be rid of us. Tonight we will either be recognised for who we are and accounted for or forced into a battle that it would be difficult to win. Will you help me?'

Andalus begins a slow rocking motion on his heels. He holds his hands in front of him, stares at the ground, his face blank, and does not speak.

I am not surprised.

'I too have not spoken properly, Andalus. What I have to say is difficult. I have not asked for what I really want. I too cannot speak. Why is that?

'Tonight I will though. I have to. You must help me.'

'Speak.

'Speak.

'Speak.'

He does not. I stand up, take a deep breath, walk over to him. I grab him by the coat he still wears and draw him to me. His eyelids flicker open. I speak in a low voice. 'You will not live another week in this place. They will come for you. I know these people, what they are capable of. They will come for you and drag you from your hole, slit your throat and bury you in a shallow grave beyond the walls. The weakest are the most dangerous. I am your only hope.' I let go, pushing him back down at the same time.

He moves his lips. I lean in to him. 'What? What are you trying to say?'

Nothing.

I give him a sharp kick in the leg.

I feel him staring as I leave.

I walk quickly, straight at the man in the alleyway. At the last second he moves to one side.

I feel light-headed and walk to the kitchens to eat. There is no sign of Elba. I do not ask after her. There is no one else eating.

When I am done I go to her flat. There is no one home. I try the handle. It is locked. I think about leaving the toy but I cannot be sure Amhara will get it. I want to place it in her hands. I start down the stairs. As I do, as I walk past the weeds in the cracks, the splintered wood on the rail, something hits me and I have to stop. I hear Tora. I stop in mid-stride and turn my head, listening for the sound again. I look at where it came from. But I know, knew straight away, it is not Tora. It is her voice dragged up from memories. Her standing in the door, waiting for me, a smile on her lips. This time a smile. Her wanting to see me. A moment twenty years ago when I made her happy. And it hits me. I can see her. She stands there and all that separates us is two decades. To say it is nothing. But it is too much.

I see a figure at the corner of the street. I walk towards him and he vanishes.

I go back to the houses. That is all there is to do now. Look for more proof. Tonight I will ask for what I have come for. I will find a way to free Tora. I cannot now. It is too light. I must just hope they give me a chance later on. Perhaps what I ask for will change everything. Perhaps it won't.

I follow the sun. As it moves overhead so I move through the town. I knock on door after door. Time after time they remain closed.

I realise I am completely alone in the streets. The children have gone. I turn around. I scan the tops of the houses. I watch clouds cross the line made by the rooftops. I scrape my foot along the sand. There is only silence. If someone is following me they are keeping themselves well hidden. I turn around and around with my arms held out, my face to the sky. I feel the breeze beneath my arms. Grey buildings. Sunlight. Shadow. Dust blown into eddies.

Door after door.

At dusk one opens.

The man is blind.

And I know who he is.

He was another official in my administration. He ran the Farming Licensing Department. I stare at him.

'Who's there?'

I reach out to him. I fold him in my arms. 'Thank you,' I say. 'Thank you.'

He struggles now. 'No.' His voice barely registers.

'It is me, Bran. You know me. We used to be friends.'

'No.' He struggles. He is like a fish before I beat it against a rock.

'Bran.'

'No. They will come for me. Please.'

'You know me. How dare you deny me? I made you what you are.' I speak softly.

Through his chest I can feel his heart beat. His ribs feel brittle. Like if I squeezed hard enough they would snap.

I put my face against his. My face is wet, my mouth at the bridge of his nose, my teeth sensing the taste of his flesh. I breathe over his blind eyes.

I push him away. He falls down. He whimpers.

Back at the shelter I find that Andalus has gone. I am not surprised. I walk through a few of the streets around the alley but there is no sign of him. I will not look for him anymore. Chances are he will not be of much use.

It is well after sunset when I walk into the courtyard of the town hall. In the middle stands the Marshal dressed, rather strangely, in a long white gown. 'Come in,' he says. 'The others are here. We can begin.'

I follow him into the hall where we had our discussion about the names on the wall. Seated at a table in the middle of the room is Elba, who has her back to me. The man who has been watching me stands in a corner of the room. There are three empty chairs at the table. The Marshal extends his hand towards one of them, motioning for me to sit.

He goes over to talk to the man, whom I assume is a soldier. I whisper to Elba, 'Hello,' I say. 'I am sorry about the other night. My behaviour was inappropriate for the circumstances.'

She does not look at me but says, 'You should not apologise for who you are.'

I do not get a chance to respond as Jura returns and sits down at the table.

He asks, 'Where is your friend?'

'I could not find him. He must have gone for a walk. He probably wouldn't have been good company. He is not very talkative.'

'So you say.' Jura rests his hands on the table but says nothing more.

'Well?' I say.

He smiles at me. 'We have a lot to talk about.'

'We do. Why have you called me here? You said you had come to a decision. What is it?'

'In time, Bran, in time. First we must wait for the other member of our party.'

'Who is that?' But I know already.

'A man who wants to talk to you. We tried to persuade him not to. But it is his decision. This is his town.'

I feel the skin at the back of my neck prickle. 'Who?'

I hear footsteps behind me. I don't want to turn around.

I feel a hand on my shoulder. I look at it. It is white, manicured, the nails clean.

'Hello Bran.'

I mumble. It is not how I want to sound. 'Abel.'

He sits down opposite me. We stare at each other. The old warrior and his friend, his foe. He has half a smile on his face. He is tall. His limbs spill over the chair, over the table. I note the creases in his face, the grey in his hair, the paleness of his skin.

The years I have known this man. The things we have been through, the things we have seen. At this point, seeing him, I am numb.

The room grows darker. No one has lit a candle. Elba gets up to do so, sits down again.

He speaks first.

'I want to hear your story, Bran. I want to hear why you are here.'

'Hello Abel. Friend.' I look at his eyes. Paler than I remember.

Abel stares at me. He does not blink. Then, again: 'I want to hear your story.'

'Just as I want to hear yours. I have many questions.'

'So I have been told. You have come to us with fantastic stories, calling us murderers. You claim to have journeyed here across the oceans, a survivor, a wanderer.'

I feel a chill. 'Are you continuing the game? You too.'

'I'm sure I don't know what you mean.'

'You know me.'

He says nothing for a while. Then, 'What do you want?'

'If I tell you, will the games stop? Will you acknowledge the truth of who I am?'

Abel makes no movement.

I grip the table. 'What is going on? I have come with a plausible story about Axum. You all know who I am. Yet no one will admit it. You all stay out of my way, do not look me in the eye. It is like you are trying to persuade me I do not exist. Have never existed.'

The half-smile returns but still he says nothing.

I lean back. 'Very well. We can play your game for a while longer. I have more proof of who I am now.'

'More?'

I have brought my bag with me. In it I have placed the jacket and the letter. I have left the portrait in the shelter.

'I told your assistant about these,' gesturing in the direction of Jura and placing the items on the table.

Abel takes the letter and reads it. The smile disappears again.

'An item of clothing and a letter you could have written yourself. Hardly proof.'

'It is not my handwriting. I found it in your house.'

'So you say.'

'We both know who wrote it. Why would I make this up?'

He does not answer but says instead, 'You have broken into a lot of places. You must think us a very lenient people. Perhaps you think us lazy. Slow. Dog-people.'

I stare at him. 'I have found my portrait as well.'

For a moment he looks almost startled. 'Portrait?'

'My portrait. A portrait painted when I was younger, when I was the Marshal.'

'When you were the Marshal.' My old friend appears to have adopted the habit of repeating what I say. Perhaps it gives him time to think. 'A portrait of you?'

'Yes.'

'That is strange. Where did you find it? Was it in the hut in the orchard?'

I stare at Abel wondering if that is another joke. 'Where I found it is of no concern. The fact that it exists is what is of concern, what should be of concern to you.'

'And what does it look like, this portrait?'

I do my best to suppress a smile. 'Why, like me of course. Only younger.'

'I mean,' says Abel – I have unsettled him – 'I mean, how were you portrayed? What was the pose? What was the condition of the painting? Tell me more about this painting of you.'

'I am in uniform. Three-quarter profile. Though the colours are faded you can see that I am portrayed as a leader.'

'Faded?'

'Yes, it was painted a long time ago but that is of no concern. It is in reasonable condition.'

'And you're sure it's you?'

'Of course I am sure. It is me, clear as daylight. There is an inscription under the portrait. True, that is faded more than the painting but a closer look would reveal a name, my name.'

'What makes you certain? You say it looks like you but is it you? Was it you? When was it painted would you say?'

'Fifteen, maybe twenty years ago. Not long enough for your argument to be valid. It was the portrait that used to hang above my desk – your desk now. There is still a darker patch where it was hung. Perhaps you had it replaced with one of yourself. You accused me of vanity.'

He waves this away. 'But still, a long time. Long enough for appearances to change.'

'For the painting to change? Paintings do not change. That is why they are commissioned.'

'Exactly. But you have changed, no doubt. You looked one way once and now you look another perhaps. You say you lived on an island. Did you have a mirror? Have you seen yourself recently? Would you recognise yourself? You can show me the painting. You can say here I am. See me. You can see it is me. And yet how can I see it is you? How can I who do not know you see that a twenty-year-old faded painting is you as a younger man? I do not know you. You say you know yourself but I do not know that, that has not been proven to me. The painting is not your proof. You must look elsewhere and find other proof.'

I bang the table. I shout at him. 'You may despise me, Marshal Abel! You may despise me but you cannot deny me. You especially. You betrayed me. Twice. You banished me. I stayed away for years. And I survived. You were hoping I wouldn't. I survived. I lived. I thought. Ten years alone with only memories. Memories like ghosts. Ghosts everywhere.' I stop myself.

'Then I come here at great danger to myself. Not only the voyage but just by being here I risk death. I bring a man to you, a man whose presence means danger to the settlement you stole from me and you deny everything. You offer nothing.'

I open my mouth to continue but before I can, Abel asks softly, 'What do you want from us?'

I get up quickly from the table.

'I want …' I breathe in quickly. I do not look at Elba who is staring at me. 'I want a retrial. I want to be judged again in the light of the current events and those of the previous ten years. I do not want revenge on you. I do not want to be Marshal again. I do not seek to accuse you once more of participating in the murders for which you held me accountable. I want my legacy re-evaluated, my crimes recognised for what they truly were and my efforts in bringing an enemy General to the settlement authorities at great personal risk to myself noted. I want to be allowed to live among my people, the people I helped create. Failing that, give me an end. Death, at least, brings redemption. Don't deny me an end.'

There is silence.

'I want to know what has happened to my friends and colleagues. I want to know if Tora is still alive, the woman I loved.' I look at Elba but she is still staring at the table.

'Whether or not she loved me well enough, I still want to know what has become of her. And ...' Here I pause and feel my voice tremble slightly. 'And I want the executed to be remembered. There is no monument to their sacrifice. The hundreds we had to kill, they should be remembered too. There were nine hundred and seventeen of them, Abel. Nine hundred and seventeen. Forgive me, please. I have to be forgiven. Please. They come to me at night. I cannot shake them. When I shut my eyes I see them. When I open my eyes they hide behind trees, on cliff tops, in the shadows. Every moment I see their faces, some of them. Others just blank. Skin. I have searched and searched for the names but I cannot. I cannot. Please.'

Abel's jaw is set in a firm line. 'You want to be re-judged? How can one be re-judged? One judgement is enough, surely? A judgement determines right or wrong. If the judgement was incorrect there would be no judgement in the first place. You cannot be re-judged. You ask the impossible.'

I am quiet for a while. 'Do you admit you know who I am? Do you admit ten years ago a trial was held in this very room at which the citizens of this town banished me for life to the far corners of Bran territory?'

'I admit no such thing at all. Nothing. There was nothing.'

'Nothing? But look what has come of nothing,' I say, pointing to myself. I am shouting again now. 'Somehow I have appeared from nowhere, no one will admit to having known me and yet I know so much about this town. Of course you recognise me. I can see it in your eyes. You are just afraid to admit it. You are afraid of what that might mean for the paradise you have built. The paradise you have built on the bones of the dead.'

I am out of breath now. 'In spite of your best efforts I have gathered proof of my past, the most obvious being a portrait of me. You refuse to admit it for fear that you might have missed something, for fear that the past you buried has resurfaced. I come here, searching for the forgiveness I cannot live without,' again my voice trembles but I plough on, 'yet you will not look me in the eye and allow me to explain, allow me to say what it is I need to say.'

'You have told your story, old man. You have taken up much of my time, much of our time, telling your story. We have given you charity and friendship but it is not enough for you. We have given you shelter and food but it is not enough. We have allowed you to be part of the present and the future of this town but that too is not enough. Instead you must have forgiveness as well. For what? For the story of your past? A past that implicates this town? Forgive you? Why would we forgive you if it makes us guilty? You have not accounted for that, have you? And indeed, how can we forgive you if we do not know who you are? Not knowing who you are we cannot forgive you for the crimes of which you say you and all of us are guilty.' Abel's voice has risen.

'And your friend the General,' he continues, 'You go on about a General you have brought to us. Where is he? Is he at this table? I don't see him. I have never seen him. A General who doesn't speak? We do not know of any Andalus. He does not exist for us either. He, the Axumites, gone.'

He is screaming now, leaning towards me, screaming. 'Show him to me! Bring out your exhibits. Why isn't he at this table, voice or no voice? Is he one of your ghosts, your stories, your lies?'

He stops. He is breathing heavily. The room is silent.

I go on, quietly. 'We did not know what we were doing. It is important I am absolved. I have no life without redemption. You have condemned me to something beyond pain. You too need to atone.' I take a deep breath.

'Abel, the children were the worst. The sick, one born without a hand, one born simple. There was a boy aged seven. I went to his cell late at night while he was sleeping. I sat at the foot of his bed and wept. Why could I not say that before? Why could I not admit it? At dawn I left his cell, went to my office and gave the order for him to be hanged later that day. You may remember they had to carry him there because he was too weak to walk. You may remember the father bursting into my office, attacking me and the soldiers defending me. They hit him so hard, so hard, so many times that we had to hang him the day after his son. The soldiers carried him out and I locked the door. I pulled my knife out, held it to my neck. I thought of what was happening to him, to his son. I thought of duty. I thought of the future. I put the knife away.'

Elba turns away, puts her hand to her mouth.

'Why did we do that, Abel? Why didn't we just allow the boy to die in his own way?'

Abel is silent for some time. He stares at me, then down at the table. 'Never being able to be one thing completely, sometimes that is the greatest sin. Is that you, Bran? Somewhere in there a good man but one too concerned with ideas.'

'Forgive me or execute me. I cannot go back to the ghosts. We used to be friends. I am asking this one thing of you.'

I am saying too much. I did not mean to lose control.

Speaking more softly now, Abel says, 'We are not an unfeeling people. My good friend Elba,' he says, nodding at her, 'tells me you have struck up a relationship with her daughter. She says she likes you too in spite of your strange ways. We will offer you another life. On one condition.'

I look at him. 'You know she is my daughter.'

His face darkens and his fingers curl but he ignores me. He goes on, 'On the condition, on pain of death, that you give up these stories for ever, that you give up trying to drag us down with you, that you embrace who we are now, not what you say we were.'

'Why?'

'I have told you. This is a new world. We will not begin it as killers.'

'What am I if I am not who I say I am?'

The Marshal looks hard at me. He sighs and Elba looks away. He is silent for a while. Neither of us speaks. At last he says, 'We will not remember you.'

With that he gets up from the table and walks out the door. Over his shoulder he says, 'You have until morning to decide.'

I am left alone with Elba. I look over at her. She is silent. I sit with my head in my hands. Eventually I look up again and find her looking at me.

'Why do you make everyone angry?'

I ignore this. Instead I ask, not looking at her, 'What I said about Amhara. It's true isn't it?'

She is silent.

'It is, isn't it? She is Tora's daughter by me. She is the right age. She has my eyes. She could have been conceived the last night we were together. Before she went completely over to Abel. And you are a friend of Tora's and not the child's mother.'

'She is yours if you want her to be. You have a role to play here. You can be a father this time round. The condition still stands.'

I sigh.

She reaches over the table and takes my hands in hers. 'Give this up. Give up your search. Give up your stories about the past.'

'Why do you say things like "this time round" if you don't believe me, if you don't know my story is true? Why can't you admit it?'

She shakes her head. 'Surely there are more important things than your guilt?'

I look down at the table. 'Thank you,' I say. 'You are very kind and I know you mean well.' I pause. 'If you'll permit I would like to show you what I was going to show you earlier.'

'What is it?'

'We will need to leave. It is a short walk away.' I stand up. 'Come.' I hold out my hand to her.

The night is cold. Elba shivers and I put my arm around her. I lead her into the alley.

'Where are we going?' She asks. She sounds frightened.

I do not answer but take her by the hand again. She holds back a little and I find myself walking slightly ahead, gripping her hand.

'You're hurting me.'

'You must come here. You must come with me.'

'Tell me what you want to show me.'

'No. You must see it first. See it then judge.'

'See what? It is dark. Black. There is no moon. What is there for me to see?'

She pulls and her hand slips out of my grasp. I turn back and reach for her arm. It is soft, thinner than I imagined. The bones of a bird. I look at her. She has a grey face. Grey like the light. I pull her. She stumbles. I pick her up. She is so light in my arms. So light. I pick her up as I would a sack, place her on her feet again. My fingers are deep in her flesh. Her mouth does not move, hangs open in the light. I edge her along the alley wall, my hand on the skin, skin like paper.

'What are you doing? Please.'

We are lovers in a dance. I hold her close.

I turn her around, still holding her arms. I pull away the canvas from the shelter and feel for the portrait. She slips away and begins to run. Three steps and I have her. Her arm behind her back. 'You will look. You will look now.'

I kick away the rest of the tarpaulin and there it is. The paint, some-how, brighter. A glow from behind the skin, behind the eyes. I hold her with one hand, my grip tight. I reach down and pick up the portrait.

'Look,' I whisper. 'Look at the man before you.'

I can see her face from the side. 'What?' She half turns. Her voice is frail.

'What do you see?'

'Nothing.'

'What do you see?' My voice changes. It is not mine.

'Nothing.'

I take her jaw in one hand, squeeze. 'Why do you see nothing? Look at me. Why do you see nothing? Is there nothing to see? Nothing to fear? From your Marshal? You are afraid of him. You are afraid of these people and their disregard for the past. I can see this in you. I can see fear in you. The whole town is afraid. They stay indoors because of what might happen to them if they show knowledge of me.'

I shake her. She closes her eyes. I shake her again. Her head lolls from side to side as I shake. There is a tear. I hold her face between my hands. I wipe the tear and it makes furrows in the dust from my hands, the dust on her face.

'Go then.' The voice, deeper, still not mine. 'Go then.' I shove her away.

At the entrance she turns to me. I can barely see her. A grey cloud. She speaks softly. I strain to hear. 'She told me you were like this. She felt everything for you: love, hate, fear. Everything. You were impossible to love unconditionally. You. You are the one who did not see. Who would not see.'

She turns away again. She floats away from me, slides into the dark.

I have no time to lose. I grab a heavy stick from the ground and make sure I have my knife on me. I run to the town hall. At the entrance to the courtyard I stop and press in to the shadows. There is a guard on the door. I will him not to see me. I walk round the circumference, still in the shadows. It works. I am almost on him when he notices me. He holds up his hands but I am already swinging and he goes down at the first blow. I run up the stairs.

At the door I am breathless. I shout, 'Tora.' I shout it three times. I lean in to the door, press my ear against it. And I hear an answer. One word. It is soft. Just one word. 'Bran.' But, this time, I know it's her.

'Tora.' I barely mouth it. I have found her.

Then there is shuffling behind the door, people struggling perhaps. I run with my shoulder at the door. It does not budge. I use my knife to try and pick the lock but nothing again. I take the stick and begin to pound the door. The blows glance off. It is far sturdier than others. It is as if something is pushing from the other side, warding off my blows. I press my ear to the wood but the noises have stopped. 'Tora?'

Nothing.

'I will come back. I will find an axe.'

I run downstairs, out the door. The man has disappeared.

I do not get very far. At the entrance to the courtyard there are men. They carry spears and a rope.

My time is up.

The man I hit is amongst them. He walks up to me, holds up his hand to my neck. He takes it, gently at first, then squeezes hard. I do not flinch. He says nothing, just winks. He steps to one side and motions for me to go.

I am taken to a prison cell, the same I was kept in ten years ago. The walls are made of stone. When the door is shut behind me it is completely black. I sit against the wall, pull my knees up to my chest. I lean my head back, open my eyes. I watch as the shapes float towards me, appearing at the corners of my vision. When I turn to them they vanish. Forming and reforming in the black light. I let them come to me and do not shut them out.

Later I am turned towards the wall. I hear the wooden shutter in the door open and Elba's voice. 'Bran.'

After a minute I get up and go to her.

There is silence between us. We just look at each other.

'There is still time,' she says.

I drop my eyes from hers. 'Amhara.' I do not know what I want to say. 'Tora.'

Her voice rises a little. 'Bran. You do not know what will happen if you go.'

I reach through the shutter and hold her face in my hand. I squeeze lightly and she leans into it this time. A figure standing back in the dark reaches for her and moves her away. I watch as the blackness swallows her. She is gone.

No one else appears. I do not sleep. They do not feed me and I drink nothing. I wait for what is coming.

The door opens almost a day later. Two soldiers take me by the arms and lead me out. The cells are at the rear of the administrative complex. I come out of the courtyard. It is dusk.

And now they have come out. All my people have left their houses. They line the streets, some arm in arm, some holding the hands of children. Some look at me, others at the ground. They all have blank expressions. Doors to the houses are open.

It is silent. Hundreds of people and it is quieter than it has ever been. I walk slowly onwards. The soldiers, pressing close behind me, make it clear I am heading for the gates.

I scan the crowd for faces I know. I see many. I do not see either Tora or Elba. But I catch a glimpse of Amhara. Just a glimpse. She is watching me, biting her lip. None of the people I know acknowledges me. As I walk past, the crowd closes in behind me and follows me to the gate.

I am reminded of how I felt entering the town a few days ago. I imagined then crowds of people I could not see parting to let me through, staring at my back when I passed. Now I see them.

As I get closer to the exit I see Abel standing in the gateway, flanked by the wooden pillars. He holds out his hands to me, takes me by the arms, leans in and kisses me on both cheeks. He is saying goodbye. He says nothing. He nods his head to one of the soldiers, who pushes me forwards. We walk out of the town, Abel next to me.

'Why?'

Abel stops. He leads me by the arm out of earshot of the soldiers. 'Surely you know?' He whispers.

I almost feel like laughing. Instead I ask, 'Why did you not have me executed in the first place?'

'It would not have been right.'

I do not say anything. It is too late. Suddenly I realise I do not want to die. And, I am afraid of going back to the island. I do not want to go back there.

'Where are you taking me?' I ask gruffly. Abel says nothing.

'You mean to hang me,' I say. 'You mean to hang me in the orchard within sight of the hut. This much I know. You are too scared to give me my public trial, my retrial,' I correct myself, 'because you fear the past. You fear what cannot be undone. I appear to have bred a successor and a community of people who have become ashamed of their origins.

Face me, for I am in all of you.' I yell this so the crowd can hear.

Abel grabs me by the shirt. He whispers, 'All your talk of paradise, of better ways, of a once-again powerful human race, and now you want to crush it? You say we are afraid of the past but what of the future? What is it you want, Bran? Do you know?'

I do not say anything.

He laughs, 'You caught me off-guard at first when you re-appeared. I have some repair work to do now. I may have erred by not killing you when we first saw you climbing the mountain. But you cannot kill ghosts, at least not in the open.'

He lets me go and whispers again, 'Make-believe. How does it feel to be make-believe.' It is not a question. He pats me on the shoulder. His hand lingers for a second.

He drops it and strides off towards the town.

'Wait!' I call out. 'My daughter. Amhara. What have you told her about me?'

Abel stops and turns to me. 'Your daughter knows nothing of you, Bran, and will never know anything of you. She is our future now.' He turns again and walks off.

I watch him go. He is a way off now, walking back towards the town. Only the two soldiers accompany me.

And then I see her. There amongst the people, two rows back, lit by torches. It is her. It has to be. Someone I know so well, someone who was such a part of my life: a friend, a lover, a traitor. 'Tora!' I shout as loud as I can, 'Tora!' The faces in the sea of people stare straight at me and I know it is her. She is far off but it has to be. Are there people holding her back? I shout to her again and now I try to run. I try to run through the soldiers but they block my way. I struggle through their grasp and am clear to the town but one trips me and puts his boot into my back and I taste dust in my mouth. I wriggle almost free and am on my feet again but one of the soldiers draws back his fist with his hand gripping my throat and that is all I remember.

12

When I come to it is dawn. I can taste blood and dust and I cannot breathe through my nose. My eye is swollen and I have grazes along the side of my face. Looking back towards the town I can just make it out in the distance. There is a trail leading across the sand from where I lie. I realise they have dragged me almost a mile away from the town. Though I can barely make it out I believe the gates have been closed and the people are gone.

After a while I notice that there are more tracks than just mine and those of the two soldiers leading away from the town. They are fresh. People must have passed me in the night. One set of tracks is like a furrow. As if someone was being dragged. Tied-up. I follow them.

I don't recall the first moment I notice them.

Out of the white noon light they appear, not suddenly but as if by osmosis. A mirage. My legs give way.

I do not speak. I do not think.

Then I get up and run. I start to run towards the tree, the one where

Andalus and I stopped, the one where Tora and I spent those hours together years ago.

Andalus stands beneath the tree. I jog up to him. He stands with his back to me but I am not looking at him. I stop a few metres away. He is looking up at the tree. As am I.

He stands looking up at the body hanging from the dead branches of the tree.

A sound escapes my throat.

Tora. My Tora. She looks the same as she did all those years ago when last I saw her on the beach, looking after me, the salty breeze in her hair.

All I can hear now are waves, like the ocean over the mountains.

There is a drop of blood in the corner of her mouth. A bit lip. A punch. Vomited up from the throat.

I am sorry. I am sorry.

She swings slowly from the branch.

Andalus stands still. He is fading away now.

I feel for my knife. I do not have it.

I reach out for Tora's legs. I hold on to them. I sniff them. They still feel warm. They smell like her. Like living flesh. I look up at her. The sun, filtering through the branches, blocks her face. She is just a few hours dead.

Another sound from me.

I pick up a stone. I climb into the tree and saw through the rope with the stone. It takes a long time. Her body falls to the ground. Tora's dress covers her face, her legs naked, dead.

Andalus does not move.

I get down from the tree and go up to him. I put my hand on his shoulder.

And then I hit him. I still have the rock in my hand that I used to cut down Tora. I lift up my arm and hit him on the temple. He sees it coming. He does not struggle. I watch his eyes as I bring down my hand upon him. I watch his eyes, and they widen but he does not scream, he does not say a thing. Again and again I hit him. Some blows slap against blood – a stone dropping into a pool. Some blows miss altogether. More and more miss. After a while there is no more sound. Nothing. And there is nothing in my arms, nothing at my feet. Just nothing.

I fall to my knees again. Then roll over. I am breathing heavily. I cover my face with my arm.

I lie there for a long time.

I stand up.

I stand up and walk away. I do not stop for two hours.

Then I go back.

I go back to the tree, back to the body. There is just one. Where Andalus's should have been is nothing. No blood. No body. Nothing.

I understand now. What he was.

Or, I already understood but did not know I did. Did not admit I did.

I scrape out a hole in the dirt. I place her in it. I cover her with rocks, starting from her feet. I look at her face with every stone I place on her. I do not hurry. She looks peaceful. Her skin is grey, tight. She looks dead. A bug crawls from her mouth. I bury her facing upwards, naked, open to the earth. It is our custom.

I lay down next to her. The night draws in and I wrap my coat around me. I feel beetles scraping at my ears. I sleep fitfully, shivering. I dig into the earth with one hand. It is warm. I lie asleep with one hand buried and the dust sifts over me.

In the morning I see them. Twenty, thirty of them. They are far off. They shimmer. Disappear, re-appear. They carry sticks, clubs, spears.

I begin to run.

Whenever I look over my shoulder I see them. I dare not stop nor think. I grab fruit from trees as I jog past. I drink heavily at streams. The black bodies on the horizon chase me onwards. At the top of the mountain I see them spread out in the plain below. From the bottom I see them at the top, each one silhouetted against a white sky.

I sleep. I have to. But only for a few minutes at a time. I sleep on my haunches.

I run.

I run until I reach the shore and I put out to sea.

I watch them line the shore. They stand still. They do not gesture at me. I can see their eyes.

I watch them until they are over the horizon.

It is thirteen days since I arrived.

13

It is like coming home. I cannot deny it. The island, I want to say, looms out of the mist as I approach. But it does not loom. It floats to the surface of my vision early one morning as I lie in my almost becalmed boat.

A home I wished I would never see again.

It has been a hard crossing, a hard time of it. I left with little water, without catching any food. I grabbed as much fruit as I could. I have had one a day. The last were shrivelled. There was one fish left in the boat. It was covered in mould. Three days off the coast it began to rain. That saved my life. I collected water using the sail. I tied a line to the side of the boat. Once a fish was enticed to the bare lure.

If I passed over the ruins and the statue again I did not notice. I was completely on my own.

I set my course due east. I did not expect to hit the island. Even with a compass, finding a small patch of turf in this immense ocean is a miracle. The island, it seems, has brought me home.

I feel my heart beat a little faster as I get closer. I think of the marshes, of the peat bogs, of the forest. I think of the quiet here, broken only by the occasional gull. I think of my cave, empty now.

I approach from the side of the cliffs. Their collapse has not halted while I've been away. Great swathes of rock and mud have slipped into the waters below. I see the large white rock on the sand.

The rain has not stopped either. It is light, very light. I am not sure whether it is rain or mist.

I put to shore in the same spot from which I left eight weeks ago.

The first thing I do is dig up some roots. I eat them raw.

It is like someone else has been here. An axe and a spade leaning against the cave wall. My water container standing out in the open, overflowing. Marks in the sedge. Marks on the rock. Things are where I left them but it seems so long ago it may as well be a stranger who did those things.

The cave smells. I notice in the corners, under the grasses, fish, rotting tubers, a bowl of gruel. I do not wonder at why they are there. I think back to the ghost of Andalus. I clear the food away. I am done with him now.

I come across some of my old notes. Without an almost constant fire, they have absorbed moisture and are damp to the touch, though still readable. I think of all the tasks I have: collecting food, digging peat, making notes. For a brief time I thought my days might not end on this sinking island. But it was not to be. Now I have to work out when the end will come, whether my absence has accelerated the end or postponed it. I lean against the wall. A choke escapes my throat.

I find I am struggling to remember Elba. Tora is the one I remember. Her black hair, skin so translucent as to be grey. Eyes so dark sometimes you could not see the pupils. It is her I remember, her I think of. Her alive, I mean. I try not to think of the other. She is with me now more than ever.

I remember her standing at the shore looking after me. I remember her standing at the gate of the town, held by burly soldiers, as a fist hit me in the face. I can taste her fear. It sickens me.

And I remember Abel. I remember the night before I was arrested the first time. I remember my hand around his throat. His hoarse, harsh words, my stomach torn in two. I remember his words and my realisation that it was him, that it was all him. I remember him slumped in the chair as I left, staring after me but with eyes blazing, triumphant.

I struggle still to see the sense in it, to see the rightness of it.

I remember him in the hall three weeks ago. The same expression on an older face. The anger, the righteousness, the incomplete answers. I think back to Jura's glances to the side, the closed doors, dropped eyes, shadows in the streets. Abel all the time, pulling the strings.

A man with a vision of a new world. I trained him well. A new world with no space for the old, no space for shadows.

What did it take to order the death of Tora? At which point was it decided: my return, her letter, her word to me from behind the locked door, her compassion for me, or was it simply my presence, my refusal to disappear?

I wonder how it happened. Did a crowd of men approach with blazing torches and strong wills? Did they shout out at her? And what did they do to her? The concubine of the hated. Did they punch her? Threaten her? And when she was strung up did she cry out? I think not. I think she would have looked at the people with scorn. Brave to the end.

Perhaps she asked to go with me.

A new world, beginning like the old with a murder. The anchoring sin.

He was wrong. You can kill a ghost.

I go back to the field of stone. I stand in the middle with them all around me. They rise up again. I am in a fog of the dead. This is where they belong now. This is home.

I think of the town. It sleeps now I feel. I can hear the crickets, smell the smoke, taste the oranges. I can see Amhara running through the streets, disappearing into the shadows, Elba calling after her. I see Elba sitting, her back to me, hunched over at a table. Her friend is buried. The curtains are drawn, the house unknown to me.

I see the bodies in their graves, their bones yellow now.

What have they told Amhara about her mother?

Elba sits at the table, day after day, crying silently.

There are too many dead.

Amhara runs through the streets, her mother under the earth, the ghost of her father watching over her. The father she never knew. Though she sensed something I think. The way she looked at me when she took my hand.

She runs through the streets, runs headlong into the walls of the town, over and over again. She feels for cracks in the wall, ignoring the splinters. The streets she runs through and beyond the walls, the plains, the oceans: a small world soaked in blood. Dirty. But it is something. She makes it something. It is perhaps more than we deserve. More than I deserve.

I see her again. I am with her this time. Her and her mother. We are out on the vast plains beyond the gates of Bran. We are caught in a snowstorm. Our heads are down. I lead my wife and our daughter to a ravine out of the worst of the snow. I wrap my arms around them and my breath warms their hands. I shelter them from the cold.

There is a sudden breeze. I am on the island again, wet through.

I go back to the woods. There it is as quiet as it always was. As quiet as I remember. The chippings line the floor, still yellow and smelling of pine, as if I was here just a few moments ago. I look behind me, over my shoulder. I remember seeing Andalus, the last time I did that, sitting there on the tree stump, staring at me, staring at my back. I run my hand over the bark. It is sticky with resin.

I could sail to Axum. Seek him out. Tell my story there. But I know that will not happen. They cannot give me what I want.

It takes me a few hours to chop the wood and with it I dry out the cave. I arrange my possessions on the stone shelves. I catch a fish and haul the boat high up the shore. I don't know what to do with it. I do not need it to catch fish and I will not be going anywhere. Yet I don't want to dismantle it just yet. There is something about that, something that I cannot face. For now it must stay on the beach.

I wake several times during the night. In the morning I eat cold fish while I sharpen my blade. The spade has gathered some rust. Things weather quickly here.

I push the door open and a cold gust hits me. The island is cooler than I remember. I pull my coat closer and set off down the hill.

I smell the grasses, feel the wet strands brush against my skin, soaking me. My spade I sling over my shoulder. The soft rain trickles down the shaft and down my back. I shiver.

I think when I am out there, down in the sea of wet grass, I think. I realise why I have never planted crops, why I have never cultivated the grasses and roots to ensure a more plentiful supply. I did not plan on staying forever. Through my ten years in exile I was always going to go back. I just did not know it. The inevitability of guilt.

Soon I am at work slicing into the turf. The water running down my back changes from rain to sweat. I take off my coat, laying the spade in the bog. I watch as steam rises from my skin. I feel a tightness in my chest. It has not taken very long for me to lose strength and fitness. I look at my forearms. The veins bulge. I see the same skin, the same moles, the same scars that have been with me for so many years.

It is like I am doing it in slow motion when it happens. I have drawn the spade above my shoulders. I know precisely where I need to cut. I throw it down into the peat and water from the spade flies off into my face, into my eyes and the blade cuts through water and into something that straight away I know isn't peat. I fling the spade from me onto dry ground and drop to my knees. I reach both hands into the water and feel around in it and close the thing in my hands and draw it out, the water pouring from it in torrents down its forehead, through its eyes and nostrils, mud slaking off its cheeks. It all comes out as easily as that. I reach into the water. My one hand finds a head, the other an arm and I pull and the torso lifts free of the water like a child drowned and the water pours from it. There is too much water in the body.

I lay it on the grass. My heart is beating wildly. The body is complete. The spade has sliced through part of its shoulder but everything is there: limbs, hands, head. The body is brown, the colour of peat. It has hair, stained reddish-brown, again the colour of peat. Round its neck is a noose of some kind.

I stare at the man. There is only the noise of gulls. And then he moves. Or rather the eye does. An eyelid slides partly open. I jump to my feet and there's a scream and it can only have come from me but I do not realise I make it at the time. The eyelid reveals an eyeball, yellowish white in colour with a black iris. It stares at the rain. I catch myself peering closer at the face and waving my hand in front of it. Stupid, I think to myself. It is just the action of the rain, the trauma of being forced from the silt, the new angle of the head. The other eyelid remains closed, seemingly welded to the cheek. As I continue looking I see something else. There is a thin line across his throat reaching from one side of his neck to the other.

How did this man die? I wonder. The noose or the knife? Perhaps the noose first then the knife for good measure, or the other way round. I look closer at his neck. It is hard to say. The noose is thin, quite flimsy, it could even be a necklace – decoration, not a murder weapon. But then the slightest thing can kill a man.

I lean in closer and sniff the body. I am only half aware of what I'm doing. It smells of peat. It smells of earth, of water, silt, mud. It smells of the island.

I don't know what to do with him now.

I reach out to his face and try to close the eyelid. It does not move. I don't want to be too rough with him. I place my hand on his forehead. I take his hand in mine. It is cold to the touch and the limbs don't move. I reach into his mouth and run my fingers along his teeth. I feel something in there, something that is not his tongue. Thinking it is a piece of wood I prise it loose. I hold it to the light. It is the tip of a finger. I examine his hands. It is not one of his own. I imagine him in a struggle. A man's hand reaches around his neck but is not careful enough. The body, in rage, in fear, grabs a finger in its teeth and bites. The man reaches for his knife and draws the line across the victim's throat, releasing his finger but not before part of it has been lost. The killer clutches his hand to his breast.

So I am not the first.

I pick up the body. I am surprised by how light it is. It is lighter than the same amount of peat would be. I wade further into the bog and let him go. He sinks slowly into the water. Legs and arms first, then his chest. Finally his head with one staring eyeball disappears. There are bubbles for a few seconds. Then the water becomes still once more. Something touches my leg – the body settling perhaps – and I jump out of the water as quickly as I can. There is no reason to fear a body that has lain dead for thousands of years, I tell myself. Out here though, in the silence, there is reason enough.

I pick up the peat I have cut and my spade. It is not as much as I wanted but I am in no mood to continue the work. I begin the walk back to the cave. After a minute I glance back at the bog. It is still. A gull has landed near where I was working and pecks at the ground.

I find myself looking over my shoulder frequently on the walk back. I don't know what it is I expect to see.

Walking up the hill to the cave I look back again. It is far away now. I shield my eyes against the rain. It is getting dark. I cannot make out the pool but I know where it is.

In the cave I stoke up the fire and sit shivering. I cough every now and then from the smoke. I lie on my bed, half awake, half asleep. Whether awake or dreaming my mind is flooded with images of the body and of the killing. There is now a group of men, a group of ten leading the victim by a rope tied round his neck down a path towards the peat bog. There is a village on the island. They lead him down the path, make him kneel. They say words, they chant, there is a struggle. It ends the same way.

He is led out, though in truth he leads himself out. His head held high, he is dressed in robes, proud of his fate. His subjects follow willingly, in awe at the bravery of the man, of the man-god. To them he is not being murdered but being sacrificed so as to rise again, to protect them from afar, to become one of the ancestral spirits who seep out of the marshes every night and hang a protective cloud over the town. Some say they hear them whisper to each other. A last minute panic when being held under water, when feeling the knife on his throat. His bravery soiled at the very last. The people silent, wondering what it means. They've never had this before: one of their chosen refusing to go quietly, refusing to do his godly duty.

A killer. A cannibal. Dragged out of the woods where he had been hiding. Beaten. Spat upon. His face contorted in rage, in fear. His were unspeakable crimes, even for that age. A last second revenge before succumbing to the waters. Was he staked to the ground to prevent him rising again? How similar the fate of killers and gods.

His face parades before me. It grins, out of fear or mirth. One eye is closed, the other open.

Now he lies beneath the water of the island, breathing silt, his wounds sutured by the mud and by time.

I am not alone. He is the true man of the island. I am just one in a line. There have been others. There will be more. It does not end with me.

In the morning I lie on my reed bed, wide awake but unmoving. I think of the settlement. I think of Elba, of Amhara, my daughter. I think of the promise of a life. Is it that bad to have to publicly ignore your past, to live as another? To be reborn another: alien, empty. It could have its merits.

I catch a glimpse of a shadow beneath the door and move my head sharply. It does not re-appear and outside it is utterly silent. A gull I think, or a greyer cloud than normal. But it is my signal. I climb out of the bed shivering.

I walk aimlessly out of the cave and down the hill. I only know I do not want to go back to the peat beds, back to the man in the marsh.

A couple of hours later I find myself at the top of the cliffs looking out onto the red sea below. The tide is out and the beach stretches a long way. The cliffs have eroded badly since I was here all those weeks ago. I have lost more of my island to the sea than I should have. The rate of erosion has increased it would seem and my island is disappearing fast. I find I am not unduly bothered by the thought.

Out on the sand, on the black sand, I see the rock, large and white, lying there, unmoving. I sit down on the grass. Or, rather, I kneel down.

Kneel first then slump to one side to sit. I watch the thing. I watch, I do not think. It is too much now. I see the white mass on the black sand and I sit on the grass watching it. Then I roll onto my back. It is still there when I sit up again. I close my eyes.

14

A shadow swims through the mud beneath me, shapeless. It forms a head, a pale eye, arms. It reaches out to me, mouth open. I jump up, brushing myself off.

The white rock is still there. I realise I must go to it.

The rock is wet and smells of the sea. Seaweed clings to the base. Around it are smaller stones partly submerged in sand. Perhaps parts of the whole. If you half close your eyes, make it darker, they look like fingers. The rock is a body in the sand. I think of the myth of the man encased in rock. This rock, if you look closely enough, if you will yourself to see it, has a face etched in it, a face that cannot speak, frozen forever.

In the end it is not Andalus. The fragile imagining of him is gone.

I sit on the sand, my back against the rock. I take hold of some of the stones, let them drop through my fingers. I am surrounded by black rocks spewed out by the crumbling cliffs. And this white one, alien, out of place. A hallucination.

I think back to the dead. The nine hundred and seventeen. Washed away like the cliffs in the rain.

I walk back to the cave, back through the rain, the wet grass, the grey light. A seagull follows me overhead. The whole way I look behind me, not at the horizon but directly behind me at the ground, the mud. I see my own prints leave a slight mark on the sedge. They fill with water. In mud my feet slip in and as I pull them out there is a sucking noise and the mud closes over them. I stand for a moment in the mud. I feel my feet sink in, mud sliding through my toes. I imagine something cold beneath them: a stone, an urn, a face. I imagine a hand reaching through the earth to try to touch me. I pull my feet out and walk on. After a few paces the marks have gone completely. I stop again. Sink again. I run this time. I run through the mud till I reach grass and am not sinking. I bend over to catch my breath. I should not be shivering like this.

In the cave I build up the fire and sit in front of it, not caring about the smoke. I sit in front of it till the steam rises from my clothes. To a stranger it might seem as if I am melting. But there is no getting dry here. Not completely. If my front is dry, my back is wet. If I turn around the wet air gets to work again. There is no keeping the water out. I curl up on the bed of reeds and close my eyes.

I wake in the middle of the night to a banging on the door, a loud relentless knocking. I get up, still hazy from sleep and go to the door. I am frightened and expecting I know not what – a stranger? A friend? – but I do it anyway. There is no need to be afraid though. The wind has got up and the door is banging against the stone. There is no one outside. Still, I find myself saying hello to the dark. It sounds strange to talk.

The wind is new. It does not often get like this. Only once or twice in the years I have been here.

The next day it continues. I lie still on the mattress burning wood, peat, whatever I have. I cough from the smoke. I do not eat for the second day in a row.

I stand in front of the wall of days for hours. I have a stone in my hand. I do not add to the wall. I drop the stone.

That night it happens again. I hear the door banging in the wind. It sounds like someone knocking. I go to the door, open it and say hello. When I do this the wind seems to slacken.

In the morning I take my fishing rod and walk to the shore. I position myself so I face the cliff as much as possible. Even so I have to look at the line in the water every now and then and I cannot shake the feeling I am being watched, watched by someone crouching down, barely peeking over the cliff edge, his mouth close to the grass, whispering to it perhaps, whispering to me, saying what, I don't know. It is not a language I understand.

I catch a small fish, go back to the cave and bake it in the embers of the fire.

After two days of tending the fire almost continuously I have exhausted my supply of wood and peat. I know that I need to do something about it. I raise myself and set out, axe in hand. I leave the spade behind. I am not ready to return to the peat bogs. Not yet. But return I will. I know I will return. But for now the man must wait.

On the way there the going is difficult and I find myself running out of breath. Lack of food, I tell myself. I cannot remember it being this difficult. My feet are sucked in, even when I walk on grass it seems. I look down at them. When I press down the water rises to the surface. Bits of grass, mud, swim over the tops of my feet. Again

I find myself looking behind me, waiting for the earth to rise up as if disturbed by some mole-like creature the size of a man. Each time there is nothing.

I reach the forest. The ground here is slightly higher than the plains around it.

It is no longer a forest. A ring of one hundred and twenty-five spindly trees. Around them a brown carpet of needles. The trees are barely twelve feet tall. If it's done right they can be felled with just twenty swings of an axe each.

It is a place of darkness. The trees make it so.

When I stand in the middle of the circle of trees in every direction in which I face there is a potential hiding place behind me. If I look ahead, north, towards the cliffs, I sense something moving behind me. If I look south towards the peat bogs, the figure shifts to the north.

The shapes behind my eyelids will always be with me.

I look down to my feet again. If this sense of another is not imagined, then movement must take place underground. There would be a network of tunnels criss-crossing the forest, with concealed entrances. Or perhaps they cross the entire island. A legacy from the time of the smoke. Would I have only to dig to find a tunnel, a network, a whole warren of pathways, a settlement, even a city? Is there a world beneath me? One in which creatures scuttle about following the land animal they sense above them. They wait for the right moment to reach through the silt, moss, earth and drag it below. Perhaps the tunnels are filled with water. Perhaps I walk on a porous island, an island whose shell is all that is solid.

I take my axe, lift it high above my head and bring it down with all my force into the earth below. I feel it cut through leaves, earth, and then something more solid. I scrabble frantically with my hands but it is only a root. I have severed a root, clean through. Sap leaks out of the wound.

I know what I have to do, what I want to do. I pick up my axe and get to work on the first tree. I begin quickly but my grip slips on the handle and the axe flies off as I swing my arm. I stand up and see something out of the corner of my eye. A glimpse of white shifting behind the trees. I call out but hear only the echo of my voice. I have stood up quickly and am breathing heavily. Dots begin to swim before my eyes and I have to sit down amidst the pine trees. I look at the spot where I imagined the figure but nothing.

I resume. This time I am slow, methodical. I glance around me now and then. When the tree falls, I do not begin to trim the leaves and branches. Instead I begin on the next tree. And once that is gone, the next and the next. I chop through the night. I don't know how I last. By mid-afternoon the next day, every single tree is lying on the ground. I strip the branches from one and from that take as much as I can carry.

I run through the grass with my burden. I only notice my heaving chest when I am back in the cave.

I wake in the night chilled to the bone. I throw more wood on the fire and lie back on the damp grass. I draw my coat closer. I close my eyes and think of Tora. The kind words, the smiles. I think of Amhara too, running, laughing, disappearing round corners in an abandoned settlement. I fall asleep remembering Tora's warm body against mine, her head on my shoulder, her breath on my neck. This is what I see, what I feel, when I fall asleep.

It is pouring today. I strip off my clothes and run out into the rain. I run down the hill, my arms stretched out to the side to keep my balance. I trip and tumble and am up again, running again. I am a child again. After a few minutes I am no longer cold. I run out onto the flats and there it becomes more difficult. My feet begin to sink and I feel like I am in slow motion and then I am flying through the air. I land face down in the mud and I can't stop myself, my arms are useless. I am lying in the mud and I feel it breathed into my throat. I turn and retch and lie on my back. I struggle to contain my breathing. I am spread-eagled. And then I feel it happening: I am sinking.

And with the sinking I feel the hands. They prod my flesh, feeling for something to clutch. They take hold of my fingers, my hands, drag these down below the mud and they try to grab my hair but I shake my head. They grow more frantic but their hands slip off my wet limbs and I roll over again and again.

I am covered in mud now, although each time I turn the rain washes some of it away. I must look a true spectacle, white on top, brown underneath. A dissolving man.

I sit up and look around me. The grasses stretch on forever. I look over to where I have just been lying. The mud moves, as if alive. It is settling back into place. This much I know. Still, I get to my feet hastily and begin to walk away.

I walk over to the peat bogs. A short distance away I stop, crouch down. Nothing moves. I see only grass, mud, water.

I feel faint. Black dots swim before my eyes. I close them and the world spins. Lack of food. The cold.

When I open them he stands before me: shoulder wrenched from its socket, toothless jaw hanging open, wisps of red hair waving in the breeze.

And then he is gone and again I see only mud, water and the grim skies above.

I shout. I put my face close to the ground and yell with all the strength I can muster. It is not a word I yell. It is a sound, a deep guttural yell. The noise of a beast in its cave, taunted by men.

15

The man sits in a cave. He has his head in his hands. He is not in despair, merely thinking. His friends sit around him, waiting for him to speak. Eventually he says, 'The end has come. Our sacrifice will save all that we know. Though you won't be around to see it, the pain I am about to inflict will surround our settlement like a girdle, will protect our children from starvation.'

The men sitting around him bow their heads too. 'Do not forget me. I will have to live with this forever. You have chosen me to do this. I have accepted your will.' The men nod. 'We must go.'

They leave the cave in single file and walk towards the bog in the fading light. Once there, they line up, kneel down and bow their heads. The chosen man unsheathes a blade. One by one he places a hand on each man's forehead, kisses him on the cheek and slits his throat. Some tremble. None make a sound.

He rolls the bodies into the bog and drives stakes through them. It is custom. When all six have been done, the chosen man sits alone on a rock weeping. He is red, splattered with blood.

He sits alone on a rock on the wet plain and weeps. He is surprised at his reaction. He cannot pinpoint the moment he stopped believing. All he knows is that he no longer believes.

He walks slowly back to the village, the knife, still in his hand, faintly sticky.

It seems the gods listen. Things get better for the people. Fewer die. He watches his wife cook meals. He watches his daughter play. He feels glad for them. But he has stopped believing. It is difficult to touch them with his hands when he can see only blood on them. Sometimes he thinks it would have been better for everyone to have died than to have this sacrifice at the core of everything they are, everything they have become. A sacrifice he has come to think of as murder.

Though he is not a believer, everyone else is. But, is it that no matter how much belief someone has it never stands the death of a loved one? Or is it something else.

In the village people stop meeting his eyes. They shun him. Doors close as he approaches. He is shut out. He does not blame them. He feels he has murdered his friends for nothing. He does not want to live like that, surrounded by ghosts, for he knows they will never leave him.

So he does not resist when people come to his hut at night. He knows why they have come. He will take on their burden. He walks ahead of them, shivering, to the bog. When his time comes, a moment of panic.

But then as he is dying he thinks of his wife and his child. He thinks of the years to come and for the first time since the killings he smiles. It does not matter that they don't know the truth. He sees them in the streets, running, laughing, his daughter a young woman now and the sunlight is so bright the picture begins to fade slowly away.

I would have been quiet if my time had come. If the judge had decided on execution I would simply have held my arms behind me waiting to be cuffed. I would have looked the judge in the eye and not uttered a word. It befits great men to go silently to their graves.

But it was not to be.

I think again of Tora on the beach. Expressionless, standing close to Abel but not touching. I take, took, the lack of expression for pain. I think of her at the second leaving. Frightened, hauled out of her garret, pushed through deserted streets, tears running down her face, dragged through the crowds at the gate and spat on.

She would have gained some consolation from the sight of me looking at her, starting to run, before being kicked and beaten. She would have seen forgiveness. She would have seen me forgive her in that look. Though it was far away, I know she would have seen it.

Her one word to me, her saying my name, it is no redemption but I hold it close.

From some things there is no redemption. The solitude of an unfixable, unforgettable mistake.

I know that now.

I am back on the island. I am walking through fields of mud and grass. It is cold and I shiver and the rain has soaked me through. Each step is a struggle. My feet sink into the mud which sucks at and grips my feet. If I stop I sink. I cannot stop nor think. I trudge on, around the island, my feet held back, and all the time I look back over my shoulder at the swaying grass and wait for the ripples in the earth. I can sense him swimming through the mud. Eyes, mouth open, the mud flowing through him, out through the slit in his throat, the slit like a gill. He has had centuries to learn how to breathe under earth. He swims after me, long, slow but powerful strokes. He swims around boulders and roots, follows the curve of the land. He gains on me all the time, reaches out to grab my foot. I lift my heel just in time. He loses ground as he skips a stroke. He makes up ground, reaches out again. I lift my foot again. I try to run, to outrun him, to outpace him. He never tires. But I do. I am panting. With each step I seem to sink further and it is more of a struggle to lift my limbs. I do not know which way I go. I walk and walk and walk. I walk through the night. At night I lose my way and I find myself slipping into the bog and I panic and thrash out and swallow the muddy water. I hear myself cry out. I hear myself cry. I drag myself out of the peat bog and I am running now, running again, and I find myself back in my cave. I sit in a corner, my back to the wall, holding my knees to my chest, watching the entrance. Here I feel safer and slowly my breathing returns to normal. I cannot stop shivering.

In the morning I go back there.

I sit on my haunches, running my fingers through the mud. I sit for hours. My legs lose their feeling. I sway, back and forth. I talk softly to myself. I wait. I think and I wait.

Towards evening I jump to my feet. I fall down straight away as I cannot feel my legs but I get up again and stumble into the water. There is a thin layer of ice on the surface. I draw breath sharply. I reach into the water. I am up to my waist. I reach down and feel around and then my foot stands on his arm and I hold my breath and plunge down into the water. There I open my eyes but can see nothing. I grab him, one arm under his back, the other under his legs and I lift him out the water. As I lift him a gasp comes from my chest. I lift him free of the earth and

I can hear the water pouring off him, pouring out of him, leaves and twigs and water falling from his mouth. I cannot see. I feel the mud in my eyes. I blink a few times and the world appears once more, a dull blurred vision. Is it rain or the water still in my eyes I don't know but the vision, whatever it is, panics me and I am scared like I have never been. Me standing, body in my arms, choking on silt, freezing, and a moan coming from my chest that I cannot control. My chest heaves. I look down at the man, the ghost, the body. Eye sockets gaze back at me, the brown jaw, the wisps of hair, the twigs hanging from his mouth. I look back at the island and the greyness is everywhere, dusk, rain, grass, ice. I have never been this cold.

I carry him back to the cave. Once there I lay him on the straw. I set to work with the axe and a stone, stripping down and sharpening some of the branches. I bury the end of the sturdiest in about two foot of earth. I prop this up with other branches. As dawn approaches I heave the man onto it and tie him to it: his arms, torso, neck and feet. I turn him towards the sea. I look at his face. The eyes are closed. He looks peaceful. There is no vengeance in him. If anyone should approach this island this is what I want them to encounter. When my people finally come to see what has happened to me, when they come to take me back, I want them to know that I was thinking of them to the end. I want them to know that I did it for them and there is no greater love than a man who is willing to sacrifice himself for his people. And I did it for one of them in particular, a woman who did not love me as I did her. But that was fine. She gave me all I ever wanted.

At the base of the branches I place the straw man, which I have kept with me all this time, the toy meant for Amhara.

The fear is gone now. Dawn has just broken. My world is ending, grinding to a halt earlier than I calculated it would. It is acceptable that I made that mistake.

In time I will sink into the waters, my eyes, mouth open to the silt. I will become a new island man. I will wait for years, for centuries until my body is found in turn. Then stories will be told about me. Perhaps they will end well. Then I will live once more. Or perhaps just a semblance, a shadow of me. A story of me.

Outside the cave the body in the branches sways in the air. A stranger, approaching along the cliff path from my fishing grounds, might even think it alive.

Acknowledgements

Thank you to Andrew McIntosh for many a chat about the manuscript and his insight and encouragement. Big thanks to my parents and brothers for early readings and support and to Dan Hopkin for his advice. Sue Armstrong helped greatly with improving the manuscript after the first draft for which I am grateful, as I am for the support of many friends and family. Thanks to all at Umuzi and The Clerkenwell Press for their enthusiasm for the novel, and also to Karina Magdalena Szczurek and André Brink who have been extremely generous. Finally, particular thanks to my wife Tabatha who has helped most of all in this and so much else.